consequences...

Laurie Depp

consequences...

The camera never lies

*Hodder
Children's
Books*

A division of Hachette Children's Book

1

When I was little, I used to lie in bed with the curtains open, my eyes fixed on the bright, orange glow of the street lamp right outside my window, outside the cosy, warm world my mum and dad had created for me. It wasn't the noise of the cars driving past that I was interested in, or the voices of people coming into the other terraced houses on my street; just the light and the black sky beyond it. I wanted to dive out of my bedroom window into the darkness beyond the light and see what the world had to offer me.

It was beautiful and it was frightening at the same time.

And I dreamed of my future, and what my life would be like past the safety of the cosy orange light.

Then one Christmas, when I was about seven, Dad gave me a little camera, one of those point and click ones with the pop-up flash, because I had been going on at him for months about taking pictures like I had seen him do so many times on holidays. I think he only did it to shut me up. I was a talkative girl. That hasn't changed. And all I ever talked about was the way things looked, how this should be changed to match that, what went with what, how this looked better here. I loved to get everything looking just right.

Once all the excitement of Christmas had died down, I finally found the courage to take my first ever picture. I didn't want to waste that moment by rushing it. Somehow I knew it was way too important.

I was in bed in the dark, with the curtains open as usual, and suddenly flakes of grey began to flicker and dive around the bright lamp in the street outside. Quickly the snow swirled and darted, like it was burning in the flame of my light. The sky was heavy and the street silent, as the snow crept into the gaps and corners, filling them with white.

I took a beautiful picture that night, my first ever. The red button for the flash came on and I pressed myself against the cold window, training the auto focus lens on the snowy scene. Before I even looked through the viewfinder or clicked the shutter, I could already see the photograph in my mind, framed and perfectly formed, and when I was finished I didn't need to look again at the world outside the window. I knew I'd captured it just right.

Of course, two weeks later the photo came out as a splodgy brown mess. There were no snowflakes, no magical light, no brooding sky. In fact, nobody could tell what the picture was meant to show, except me. But still, I'd seen the picture in my head so clearly, and now all I needed to do was find out how to make it come to life using the camera.

I was hooked.

* * *

Now, years later, and two days after I took the picture that changed my life, I held on to the photo, kept it in my darkroom at home, refused to even touch it. It stayed on the drying line, facing the wall, away from any prying parental eyes. They never went in there anyway, and I always made sure I kept it locked, especially when I'd done a few shots they wouldn't have approved of, and I didn't want to take the risk. I didn't know what I was going to do. I was a bit shocked by what I'd photographed and a bit stunned by what I could do with it.

I went to college and did my A level coursework; ignoring the idiot boys who tried to wind me up on the bus home; chatting to people on MSN and my mobile and trying to avoid chocolate and my mum's baking.

Everything was so normal on the surface: I was Natalie. That much was the same: a bit weird, a bit quirky, depending on who you talked to. I wasn't the most popular girl at college, but then I wasn't an outcast. I had a couple of close friends who I chatted with on MSN about my 'secret'. One of them was Ravi, whose greatest ambition was to be on *Big Brother* and be the first gay Asian teenage cross-dresser to win it. Every year he got more hopeful when that series' gay cross-dresser was evicted early on.

RaviBUFF: Look Nat, you have to go for it. What's the problem? These people are publicity addicts anyway.

IMAGEGrrl: Yeah that's true.

RaviBUFF: They spend their whole lives going

3

after it. You would just be giving them some more. I should know darling. I'm dying for some *xx*.

IMAGEGrrl: You're a sad ass Rav. It's not like you ever go out in your dresses anyway. What if they get their bodyguards to come after me? Will you save me?

RaviBUFF: As if. Seriously, though. I'll do it for you if you haven't got the balls?

IMAGEGrrl: Listen, I'm the only one with the balls in this relationship Rav, and don't forget it!

RaviBUFF: OK, point taken, but even more reason you should go for it. Evie thinks so too.

IMAGEGrrl: I know, she told me. She did make me think.

Evie was the third part of our little triangle. She was like a more reliable, more sensible version of me. If even *she* thought I should sell the picture, then maybe I wasn't going to be sent to hell and eternal damnation after all.

There were times during those two days when I made myself forget about the picture that had burned itself into my mind from the moment I had taken it. But how different could things get? Surely it was only a bunch of pixels on special paper?

Deep down, of course, I knew better. It was an unexploded bomb.

And I knew I had to make a decision. Me. Nobody else.

Clive, my long-suffering Media teacher at college, was

always going on at me about pursuing proper photography. Clive was a photographer too; part time when he wasn't teaching, and he was pretty good in a 'local scenery and fairly-interesting-still-life' kind of way. He was talking about 'integrity in art' – making sure I knew how much store he set by serious, rather than frivolous, focus in a chosen craft.

'Natalie, you have to make sure you stay true to your talent, work for it, squeeze every ounce of life out of it. Never ever let yourself down by selling out for the money. There are artists and there are salesmen. You are an artist! Don't let your talent be used for anything other than art, OK? NO wedding photographs!'

I knew his heart was in the right place, but sometimes I couldn't see the difference. Tracey Emin made great art and Annie Leibovich (my hero!) took amazing pictures, but I couldn't say that what Tracey Emin did was exactly 'serious' – even if she thought so. Their pictures always looked like they'd had fun working, despite them being 'high art', as everyone said. I didn't see why you always had to suffer for your craft. What was wrong with enjoying it, too?

I would sit down hugging a mug of coffee in the photo lab at college during break and try to reassure Clive about my 'seriousness'.

'I know what you're saying, Clive, I really do, and I'll do my best, I promise.' I pretended to hide in shame the David Beckham pencil case I'd had since I was fourteen, which I now used as an ironic comment on media manipulation of young teens. 'And when I'm really famous and rich I'll make

5

sure I tell everyone who'll listen that it was you who inspired me to put the art in my photographs. Especially if I get more money for saying so.'

Clive winced and took a swig from his cup and I smiled. He looked like some old photographer from the 1960s, all long grey hair and wrinkled face. He probably didn't have a lot of money, and he'd never made his mark, artistically speaking. But he was kind and meant well.

'Do you remember what you said about that picture of the swans that I did for my Art GCSE? That it belonged on a birthday card from Clinton Cards?'

Clive twitched a hairy eyebrow in my general direction and sighed heavily.

'Now that, Natalie de Silva, was a complete travesty. You should have been shot for that. All function and no form. I'm only grateful that you've taken the right path since then and listened to me. Your photographs betray talent indeed. I hope that one day you will be coming back to see me with a magnificent portfolio, and the respect of your fellow artists. That's what you need to aspire to in our profession, believe me.'

The thing is, I did believe him in some ways. Sure, I wanted to be an acclaimed artist, get featured in the *Sunday Times* magazine for my revolutionary pictures of rock stars in their underpants, or for revealing the suffering of an undiscovered Amazonian tribe or images of war that defined a generation. I could even see myself photographing the new Marilyn Monroe in her early years, taking the picture that catapulted her to greatness.

It was just that I also wanted fame; I wanted to have the global masses look at what I'd done and know my name. Was that too much to ask?

Most photographers had to make do with a little gallery in a back street in London showing ten of their pictures to three people a day, if they were lucky. But they usually had a bit of a head start. Posh, with family money – something behind them. I came from nothing and I wanted it all.

Oh, decisions, decisions. I was sitting on a potential goldmine. A single photo could launch me, hopefully make me a fortune and let me do anything I wanted with my career. It was a picture that would be syndicated across the world, in all the big magazines, on the net, in all the newspapers: *Hello!*, *OK!*, *Paris Match*, the *National Enquirer*, all of them.

Yes, I would be flushing all my principles down the drain, and turning my back on the likes of Clive and all his integrity. But the way I saw it, I'd be like one of those actresses who does dodgy scenes in crappy TV shows, or loo roll ads, to get noticed by the big film directors. Like Catherine Zeta Jones or Anna Friel; they both started out lowly, took what they could to propel themselves forward. And look at them now. They're doing all right for themselves, aren't they? I wouldn't mind having even a bit of what they've got.

The truth was, this photo was my ticket to the future. It was time to open some doors, make some connections and use the luck that had landed in my lap when I first spotted what was happening that day in London, when I'd wandered off for a bit from the annual college Media trip.

I'd been waiting most of my life for the chance to see what was beyond the safe orange glow of home. It was time to seize the chance and get out into the big, bad world.

I contacted the newspapers and made the sale.

2

A reporter from the *Sunday Newz* interviewed me on the phone on the Thursday, and then I was called into their offices in central London on Friday to finalise the deal. I was a bit surprised about the interview. I was just hoping for the money and a few contacts, but they asked me an awful lot of questions – and some pretty personal, irrelevant ones, too. But what the hell, the reporter was so nice, he really made me feel at ease, and he seemed genuinely interested in me, and my passion for photography. So I went along with it.

And the money they offered me just blew me away. I got £150,000 up front and some syndication rights on top. Because of my age, the paper had made me sign up with an agent before they would deal with me, so I did feel like I'd got a fair deal, and I used the one they recommended: Jonathan Davies Associates. I even got the man himself, Jonathan Davies – the twenty-first-century Max Clifford, so I was told. The whole thing only took an hour from start to finish.

The deed done, the next day I prepared myself for telling my parents. I knew they would have tried to talk me out of it. Gone on about 'morality' and 'responsibility', blah, blah, blah. I couldn't take the chance of being dissuaded. I waited until Dad got in from work, and then told them I needed to talk. We sat in the kitchen, where the little de Silva family of three always had their family meetings, usually about something Natalie de Silva had done wrong. I took one of the photographs out of a brown envelope and handed it to my father. He stared at it, a bit confused at first, but then it was as though it came into focus for him, and his eyes widened, as though he couldn't believe what he was looking at.

'For God's sake, Natalie. What is this?' He and Mum looked at me, waiting for an explanation, and so I gave it to them. Predictably, they disapproved, more than disapproved, of what I had done. Dad just kept hold of the picture I'd given him, shaking his head in disappointment.

'I can't believe a daughter of mine would stoop to this. You're destroying peoples' lives – it doesn't matter whether or not they court publicity. It's not down to you to make this kind of judgement on them, is it? It's tasteless. You have to contact that reporter, and return the money. That's the least you can do right now. Limit the damage. They're not going to stop publishing it, but at least you can stand on some kind of moral platform.'

I looked at him calmly. I had expected all of this.

'Dad, I'm not some little baby, I know what I'm doing. I've thought a long time about it. This money is going to get me a career in photography. Do you really think I need A levels in Media Studies and English for that? This is my big chance and this is just the start of it.'

I kept my hands still on the table in front of me. I didn't want them to think I was nervous or unsure.

'Darling,' my mum put her hand on mine, 'what about us? We've supported you in everything you've ever done with your photography and with school and your friends, but this? This is . . .'

She seemed to run out of things to say. She just stared at the photograph on the table in front of us all, unblinking, treating it like it was a wrap of heroin or something.

For God's sake, I thought, it's only a bloody picture. If I hadn't taken it and sold it, sooner or later someone else would have.

'Mum, I can use this money to buy me a future. And I'm sorry, I respect your opinion, both of you, but I don't share it. Like I said, I'm legally able to decide for myself now . . .' I decided to use the line Jonathan had told me to say, when I told him my parents might be a bit of a problem, 'So I'm allowed to keep it.'

I've always been pretty stubborn, and today was going to be no different.

'Anyway, they're publishing on Sunday,' I forged on. 'Once it's done, they said there might be a bit of publicity and then Jonathan said he'll use that to start to set me up with some connections. It's a way in for me, can't you see? It's the best way to get into the profession and get myself known. You know it's what I've always wanted to do.'

I could see that Dad wasn't convinced. His head kept bobbing backwards and forwards. He's not the kind of father who gets mad and starts chucking things around. But I could tell he was seething. The trouble is, that's all he's ever done, and his seething has never really stopped me from doing what I want to do.

'Nat, you've gone too far this time. We've talked about this before. You're headstrong and you make choices that can get you into trouble. The damage is done now and all we can do is hope that this isn't another one of those times. I can't make you give the money back because, as you say, you're legally an adult, but what I can do is tell you what I think. I'll ask you again to give the money back and hope you decide to do so. After that, your mum and I will try to support you, despite what you've done. But you need to know that we in no way condone what you've done, far from it.'

Yes, once again, my liberal, non-confrontational parents had let me off with a mere warning. I sometimes wondered if it was because I was an only child that they were so quick to indulge me, or if they were just plain soft. They always gave me the benefit of the doubt, always wanted to see the best in me. Whatever they thought, it made for an easy life at times.

Once, in Year Eleven, I had organised a mass kidnapping of the three huge school Christmas trees, which we were going to ransom back to the head teacher for charity. Unfortunately they were all chained to the ceilings and we hadn't realised. When the bill came for the ceiling repair and glass replacement after the trees had ended up falling through the main office windows, my parents just grounded me for the evening and afterwards said that despite the damage and the repercussions, it had actually been quite a good idea really and my heart had been in the right place in thinking about charity at Christmas time. They even argued with the head against my suspension. Bless 'em. They had no idea I was only using that as an excuse to have a laugh with my mates and do something mad to relieve the boredom of school.

Another time I had my tongue pierced to add to my ear, nose and eyebrow collection. My mum started crying and ran upstairs saying she couldn't take any more and that it was the final straw. My dad just talked to me about trying not to upset my mother and the dangers of catching HIV in unregulated piercing establishments. There was an awkward moment when he suggested he might go and have a quiet word with Kev, the tattooist who'd done it, about how wrong it is to tattoo children, until I mentioned that Kevin was a very large biker guy with a bit of a temper, and Dad backed off pretty sharpish. He patted me awkwardly on the back and said I would no doubt grow out if it, 'no real harm done' etc etc. Talk about inconsistent. Still, as I said, it suited me. I could get away with murder.

3

All hell broke loose the following Sunday morning, 27 September.

It started with a couple of knocks on the door, but by eleven o'clock there were already about ten reporters and cameramen standing on the front path of our terrace. I started getting texts and calls from Ravi and Evie, and then from other reporters. Then the home phone started ringing too. I don't know how they got my numbers, but they didn't stop calling. It was just one withheld number after another. I texted Ravi to come online and then turned off my mobile. Evie was there too so we went into a private room to talk.

RaviBUFF: Oh my God, princess, have you seen the papers?

IMAGEGrrl: No, I can't get out of the house and Dad refused to order them. What's going on?

RaviBUFF: OK, sweetie, you really should see them. Your pictures are all over the *Sunday Newz* – there's even one taking up the whole of the front page, but every other tabloid has got 'your story' –

even without the pictures. There's all this stuff
about you … Actually, it's stuff you've said, as well.
What's going on, princess?

ForeverEvie: You're not going to like it, Nat.

IMAGEGrrl: What do you mean, other stuff?
There are reporters knocking on our door the
whole time and trying to take pictures. We've had to
shut all the curtains. My dad's going mad. I don't
get it. I just sold a picture … and had a chat with a
reporter. Now it's all gone off …

RaviBUFF: You 'had a chat'? Oh, princess, what
have you done?

ForeverEvie: Natalie, my dad's being going on
about it all morning. He keeps asking me why I
hang around with a girl like you. Are they out the
front of your house then?

IMAGEGrrl: Yeah. They're all over the flowerbeds.
Why would your dad say that about me? I haven't
done anything wrong, have I? It wasn't me caught
cheating with another woman!

RaviBUFF: Listen, sweetie, you'd better get on the
paper's website. You'll see what all the fuss is about
then. I'll send you the links now.

A set of blue words appeared in the conversation box.

RaviBUFF: OK, the first link is the main story.
The second is the other stuff. Don't go offline, OK?
I'm here for you …

ForeverEvie: We're both here for you, Nat, don't

forget that. And we want some of your money too, OK? (just kidding!) LOL.

Nervously I clicked on the first link. It seemed pretty harmless – it just speculated on the truth behind the pictures I had taken of Brett Ballentine. I had a quick look to check they had got the focus right and used the best angles. It was exciting. My pictures were national news! And the best one was on the front page of a Sunday newspaper! They'd chosen my favourite, where Brett is snogging the face off the woman that isn't his wife. I remembered my knees had gone a bit weak when I saw them and I'd had a split-second doubt about photographing it all. They'd just looked so in love. Nothing like the way Brett behaved with 'Trashy Kassie'. Then I thought of that girl, standing on the back steps of their house, just gawping at me. She hadn't even looked surprised, or judgemental, either, just a bit dazed, like a bunny caught in the headlights. No idea who she was, one of the Ballentine entourage I guess.

Anyway, my new agent must have got to work straight away to get all the deals done and the pictures in the papers so quickly.

Then I clicked on the second link. I couldn't believe what I saw.

Right in front of my eyes there were two full colour pictures of me, one head and shoulders in close-up, the other full-body and walking with my college books, sweeping my long, dark hair out of my eyes. They must have been taken the day before, because I was wearing my Diesel skirt and orange tights. I looked a bit windswept, but pretty good really. I wondered if I'd been airbrushed or something, to get me to look so good. My cheekbones looked great. My angles were all totally flattering. I couldn't help but smile. The power of photoshop is a wonderful thing. I certainly didn't look that good in the mirror every day.

Next to it was a headline in capitals, and an article.

TASTY TEEN SNAPPER PUTS HERSELF RIGHT IN THE PICTURE

Budding young paparazzi photographer Natalie DeSilver, from St Albans (pictured, right), has revealed the burning ambition that lies behind the controversial pictures that have shocked the celebrity world, as revealed in today's edition of the *Sunday Newz*.

Lovely Natalie, 17, has 'snapped' her way through her teens in preparation for her big break, vowing to get to the top in the male-dominated, dog-eat-dog world of the paparazzi and made a celebrity of herself in the process! Congratulations Nat, your time has come!

And now she's beating those big boys at their own game!

Natalie's already proved, with our pictures today, that she can mix it with the best of them, but the world of the paps is a tough one, where your picture is your fortune. Our young snapper also sees herself as a role model for girls everywhere.

'I'm going to get the pictures the men can't,' the beautiful brunette told the *Sunday Newz*. 'Us women can get into the places the men can't reach! I want to give the male photographers a run for their money. If I can use my feminine charm to get ahead of the game, then I'll do it.'

And as you can see, gorgeous Natalie is rather 'talented' in front of the lens, too.

DeSilver, who turns 18 next month and claims never to have had a regular boyfriend, told us she won't be afraid to use her budding sexuality either, in her search for the money shot.

'It's about time there was a girl out there, taking the pictures the world wants to see. Someone with a bit of glamour. Yes, I want to be known for my pictures, but I also want to be famous for myself. I think the world is ready for Natalie DeSilver!'

We certainly think we're ready, Nat.

And we know our readers can't wait to see a bit more of you too!

Which is why we've signed Natalie up with the *Sunday Newz* on an exclusive open-access deal, which means we will be able to see a whole lot more of our girl at every step of her trip to the top. Time for some fun for us guys too!

Natalie doesn't care about the lives she may potentially ruin, as you can see from today's exclusive pictures. This girl just wants to have fun!

'I just want the public to see the truth. If you live your life in the public eye, and earn all that money from getting your picture in *OK*! magazine, then you have to accept there'll be photographers watching your every move. And I'm prepared to do anything I have to, to get my picture.'

We can only hope she really means that!

Natalie, seen here heading to her sixth form college in St Albans, where we think she might just be studying for a diploma in 'Advanced Sexiness', is currently single, but could well be looking out for Mr Right, or even just Mr Right Now!

'I'm not keen on settling down, now or any time soon, but I would really love to date a celebrity. I've got a few in mind, so they'd better watch out: Nat's coming!'

We think Natalie's got such a great future that we'll be featuring her exploits (and hopefully some sexploits?) over the next few months, in a new, regular feature on these pages, as she unleashes herself on the unsuspecting (until today!) world of celebrity!

So, from next Sunday, exclusively in the Sunday Newz, it's 'Make a Date with Natalie DeSilver . . . Paparazzi Princess!'

Oh dear God. I crumpled down in front of the computer screen and held my head in my hands. If they were going to make me out to be some kind of slapper, at least they could try and spell my name right.

I hadn't said any of the things they had made out I'd said. At least not in the words they'd used. I might have joked with them about wanting to be famous and dating and stopping at nothing to get what I want, but . . .

And what was that about an exclusive deal? I didn't know anything about that. Featured in the *Sunday Newz*, every

Sunday? What kind of life did they expect me to be leading to fill up their pages with that kind of article?

I crawled over my bed to the window and carefully folded up the bottom corner of one of the curtains, creating a tiny triangle of light, which gave me a view over the front garden and some of the street beyond.

Down beyond my personal street lamp I could see a scrum of reporters and photographers, cameras and pens at the ready.

A little part of me was terrified and my heart leapt. I dropped the curtain back into place.

But alongside the terror, there was another cause for my palpitations. I could say it was adrenalin, but truthfully it was excitement, pure and simple. There was no turning back now. I'd made my choice, I just had to make sure I played things right. I stood up, took a deep breath and pulled the curtains wide apart. I was in full view of the reporters and photographers below me; it was only a matter of time before they saw me, waiting for them.

And I could see that the old darkness outside my bedroom window was completely gone. It was like I was seeing everything perfectly now. And it was time to step out into the light.

4

By the time I'd done my first three shoots I felt like a veteran. Everything I did seemed to turn to gold. According to Jonathan, the magazine editors loved the edgy 'youth' style of my photographs. I'd done a couple of quite formal shoots in a studio complex out in the East End, and they had led to an offer from *Style!* magazine, which I couldn't resist: not only would I be taking pictures on a top class fashion shoot, I was going to be photographed whilst I photographed, on location too. What more could a girl ask for?

On the day of the *Style!* shoot, I found myself in the middle of Trafalgar Square, with all the equipment up and ready and a crowd of tourists gathered around at a short distance, held back by a cordon of tape and a couple of flunkies making sure they didn't cross it or get in the picture.

I think London is at its most beautiful in autumn. I love the crispness of the light and the fact that most of the summer tourists have gone, leaving behind real people with real jobs, going about their business and getting on with real life. It's what makes the city so special.

The concept for the shoot was, of course, 'London'. The

idea was to get the models surrounded by pigeons in front of the fountains, so that we caught the essence of London as a powerful, living city with a vivid history. We were using the special light, even with the now clouding skies, and the grey of the pigeons and stone statues to contrast with the vibrant colour of the clothes. And they were really vibrant. They were by Nfandi Ekwo, a British/Nigerian designer who specialised in a fusion of African and British sensibilities. At least, that's what it said in my brief.

I was so busy thrilling at the prospect of having a cover photo in *Style!* by the end of the month that I didn't really care what they were fusing, to be honest. I just loved taking the pictures and being on the set.

Meanwhile, I was being photographed too, wearing some of Ekwo's 'Street Collection' for the shoot, which was a bit confusing, but exciting at the same time. Jonathan had got me on to this shoot because all of us were meant to represent a new sense of London, which in the noughties was reminiscent of how it was in the 1960s, when anything was possible and London seemed to be the centre of the world. We were proof of how anything was possible now – in the twenty-first century.

I wasn't arguing with that. From where I was standing, there was nothing about London I didn't love. I was living proof that anybody could do anything – with a bit of luck, and a smidge of talent, not forgetting an impeccable sense of timing – in this fabulous city.

'Natalie, can you lean in on this shoot, looking through

your lens but up at the sky too, so we can get your eyes reflecting the light and glimpse the cut of the neckline on your frock.'

I did as I was told. It was funny to me that an experienced photographer was recording my skill. Some of the time I have to admit that I was making it up as I went along, hoping nobody would notice. Nobody did, or at least they never said so.

I followed the instructions I was given. I was being portrayed as the glamorous, fashionable photographer who was taking London back to the world, although I wasn't sure that the world had ever forgotten how cool London is anyway. But how could I refuse?

The tourists around us clamoured for a look at both the proper models and me. It felt a little strange to be stared at for just being me, but I loved it. I knew that my life looked interesting to these people, whose everyday existence wasn't quite as glam. Why not let them have a little bit of reflected glory?

The models' clothes were a lot more revealing than mine – not to mention a lot smaller! The skirts were short: tunics and A-line shifts – to show that sixties style had returned – while the necklines and materials were very now. It gave me plenty to work with when I was back on task and not distracted by my own photo shoot.

'Sky, can you work the skirt for me? I need attitude, OK? Spikes and angles. Give it to me.' I felt like a natural.

I fired off another twenty or so frames. Before, I

used to worry about every picture, because *I* had to pay for exposing it; for all the materials, the paper, everything. Now I was like a girl in a chocolate shop and every bit of the chocolate was free and there was a never-ending supply.

Soon I had the pictures in the bag and became the main focus rather than the sideshow. I'd been in make-up already for the shooting section, but needed freshening up again for the main session.

I gave Evie a quick call while I was waiting for the shoot to restart.

'You're where?' she screeched.

'Erm, middle of Trafalgar Square. I have about thirty Japanese tourists taking pictures of me having my make-up done and talking to you. They don't even know who I am!'

'They soon will, Nat, after all the pictures you're doing and the stuff in the papers. You were even on TV the other day.' Evie was breathless. All of this was starting to become a bit more normal, partly because I had to act as if it was to everybody around me, and that took a bit of the edge off things, but I wasn't quite ready to give up 'girly loss of control' mode yet; I just had to do it without anybody really hearing me.

I whispered my excitement down the phone.

'I've got another party tonight, and Jonathan is arranging for some more modelling after today, if it goes well. Can you believe it?'

'I'm not surprised by anything, to be honest, but no, I still can't really believe it's all happening. Everybody at college is talking about it too. Déjà-vu, or what?' Evie laughed. She and I had been 'exposed' in a local newspaper for our antics on a college Media trip to Bradford a few months back. There had been some boys from another college at the Film and Television Museum and we'd gone missing with them in the middle of the city for a couple of hours instead of focusing on the exhibits we were meant to study. One of the lads in my year had told an obviously desperate young reporter, eager to get their first break, this ridiculously embellished and revealing story about me with a few additions about my sexual preferences for Asian guys. There was even a suggestion that Rav was my boyfriend. I laughed again at the thought of it. 'It must be a bit weird knowing that everyone is out to get a piece of you?' Evie said – and she sounded concerned. It didn't bother me. She didn't see the other side of it all, the life I was living now.

I didn't have time to carry on talking all day anyway.

'I'm gonna have to go, Eves, the make-up woman is back and wants my face to play with before I go back on set. I'll talk to you when I've got a bit more time, OK?'

I flipped my phone shut and swivelled back to the portable mirror stand that had been set up behind a flimsy curtain, as the make-up girl dusted my face lightly with something shiny. I saw my designer clothes and my made-up face again, glowing almost gold in the autumn sunshine. For a split second, I didn't recognise the girl in front of me: she was too self-possessed, too attractive, too perfect. Was she really still Natalie from St Albans?

I stood and moved across the concrete square to take my position in front of the lens.

I heard the whirring of the photographer's camera as I struck a pose in my gold tunic dress. Looking up, I saw the craggy front section of the National Gallery, a place I'd visited countless times, and where some of my biggest heroes had their photographs displayed. In the opposite direction was Admiralty Arch, the London sun gleaming on its ancient stonework. In between, four bronze lions guarded the base of Nelson's Column and the fountain within.

Almost without hearing his instructions, I did what the photographer asked of me, and more. I was in my own world now, and nobody could take it away from me. Tracing the shape of the column, I followed it up to the statue of Nelson itself and beyond it to the sky, raising my chin in a classic pose I'd learned right that second.

The sky was no limit at all.

5

'Nat, you need to get up now.'

I could hear the words, but they seemed to be a part of my delicious slumber and I wasn't going to give that up without a fight.

'Nat, you have to get *up*. You've got the signing at twelve.'

Through my sleepy haze I became aware of a rustling of paper and some banging about in the room. I squinted into the light pouring through the window above my bed. I really needed to get some blinds. I'd get Sarah to sort it out.

'OK, OK,' I mumbled, 'there's no need to shout. You're not my mother you know.'

I crawled slowly out of the thick white duvet, hair tangled under my arms on the pillow.

Sarah, my PA, came into sharper focus by my bed.

'Oh you look beautiful today, Natalie darling,' she seemed to be yelling. 'I'm sure the photographer will be delighted if you turn up looking like that. JD told me to get you sorted out by eleven-thirty so you're ready for the car, which gives you precisely fourteen minutes, OK?'

My focus was now suddenly crystal clear . . .

Sarah was circling the room, my bedroom, collecting clothes off the floor, replacing box lids, tidying bottles of perfume and make-up jars on to the appropriate shelves and generally doing a perfect impression of my mother. She didn't let up with her chatter the whole time. I tried to zone out the noise whilst I pulled my thoughts together.

'Sarah,' I began in a wheedling tone. 'Can I have a cup of very strong coffee.' I widened my eyes. 'Pretty please.'

Sarah stopped in mid shuffle, and smiled.

'Welcome to the land of the living, princess. It's Tuesday. Last night you had dinner at the Ivy followed by a little light drinking and a little heavy clubbing. Your pictures from two nights ago are in the *Sun*, the *Star* and the *Mirror* this morning. Judging by the pictures, you had a very good time that night as well. Glad to see you made it home alone though. Good job I sent you the taxi, eh?'

I forced myself up on my elbows.

'And one double espresso, coming up. Just make sure you're made up, gorgeous, and wearing everything on these hangers by the time I'm back.' Sarah started to go before turning to remind me. 'Oh, and it's really cold outside, so make sure you wrap up warm for the car ride.'

She gave a sarcastic wink and pointed at the open rail of clothes that occupied one corner of the large room, where one outfit had been separated from the rest. I say 'outfit' – it barely qualified as that. It appeared to be made out of sequinned strips of fabric criss-crossing over each other, in a showgirl kind of style – sort of like Julien McDonald meets

Matthew Williamson – and came with a pointless but pretty chiffon wrap thing. It had been freshly delivered from the hot young designer's (whoever that was, I hadn't registered the name when Sarah told me) showroom.

I hauled myself on to the side of my king-sized bed and stretched lazily.

It was a hard life, but hey, somebody had to do it.

6

I was in Selfridges the next day when Jonathan called me to catch up and to talk about what was happening over the next few days. He liked to keep me updated, telling me that 'an informed client is a client on message', whatever that meant. It generally meant a ten-minute chat in between make-up sessions or an interruption to an afternoon sauna. Somehow, he managed never to interrupt me when I was working.

Steven, my stylist for the morning, was very discreet. He seemed to melt into nothingness the second the call came through, leaving behind the faintest smell of some amazingly expensive aftershave. It made me wonder if he was working with Jonathan as well. Everybody else I met seemed to be, in some way or other. So, here I was, surrounded by expensive clothing and accessories, in the VIP changing room of a huge London department store; there was absolute silence, no sign of any life, around me.

'I hope Sarah's been looking after you well, Natalie. She's one of the best PAs in the business so there shouldn't be any problems.'

Sarah had started working for me a few weeks before. I hadn't understood the need for a personal assistant when everything had started to happen, but now I couldn't imagine being without her. It was hard enough getting up in the morning as a normal teenager, and now that I sometimes had work to do, or to meet people, or be looked at, I needed help with that. It wasn't what I'd expected work to be like, but I was glad of her help.

Jonathan's voice always went up at the end of his sentences, in that transatlantic way, so that even just everyday statements always sounded like questions. It was kind of soothing and made me feel like he was really concerned about me whenever we spoke. In a few short weeks he had changed my life completely and helped to get me settled into the life of a celebrity, and he seemed to know what he was talking about when it came to my career 'development'. I'd quickly learned to follow his advice to the letter. I really trusted him.

'She's great, Jonathan. Brilliant. I don't know where I'd be without her.' I paused, then added, 'She certainly doesn't need telling twice when I need something.'

It was still taking some getting used to, being a person who told other people what to do. I was only eighteen, but apart from Jonathan, it was down to me to order people like Sarah about because that's what they seemed to expect. And I didn't want Jonathan to think I was soft.

'Well it's what she's there for,' he continued in an approving tone. 'Never hesitate to ask for anything. You know that the expense account is full and you're doing very well for yourself, so you don't have anything at all to worry about in that respect. Sarah will take care of everything for you.' He paused. I could hear the clinking of coffee cups and a rustling of paperwork at the other end of the phone. Another phone rang but Jonathan continued to make me the focus of his attention. 'What are you up to right now? I hope you're relaxing and having some fun.'

'Just a bit of shopping. I'm looking at shoes for the premiere next week, but I haven't decided on the dress yet, so it's all a bit hard. I'm not used to all this you know.'

He laughed dryly. 'I know that. I remember what you were wearing the first time we met.'

'Hey, don't knock Primark, OK? It provides glamorous but affordable pieces that add context and street chic to the designer outfit.'

'OK, Ms de Silva, you don't have to *be* Sarah; just listen to her advice. And anyway, I'm not talking about the Primark. It was those clunky old biker-boots I was referring to!'

I giggled. Jonathan insisted on designer gear and high heels for most of my 'work wear'. At first it had taken a lot of getting used to, particularly the heels, but after a while I couldn't imagine why I'd worn flats for so long. Heels made me feel so slinky, sexy – they made me feel the part. And the designer gear? All I can say is I cringed when I thought of the rubbish I used to wear back in the old days – before the likes of Dolce & Gabanna came into my life. Tragic.

'OK, well just make sure the dress you choose is a

stunner, and run it by Sarah before you buy it. After the last big premiere, we got you into practically every magazine and paper in Britain and quite a few across Europe too, and the dress was the reason.'

There was a short, awkward pause.

'Well, other than yourself, obviously.' He'd almost got away with it. 'And the fact that the whole world can't get enough of you at the moment. We're turning down a lot more than we're doing, trust me. But you're going to have to do something special to beat that dress. I'll call a few designer friends and see if they have anything that will do the job.'

I twisted the back strap of one of the Jimmy Choo slingbacks I had been trying on. They were crocodile skin leather, softer than silk. I wouldn't have touched them with a barge pole when I lived in St Albans, even if I could've afforded them.

I felt a moment of self-doubt coming on.

'You don't think this is all going to come to an end, do you Jonathan? I mean, I don't really feel like I've done much to deserve it in the first place.'

'Natalie, Natalie, love, you're doing great. I've told you before, it's not about deserving it, it's about taking advantage of this world you've got yourself into. Now, we've got a couple of parties next week, one with rumours of Hollywood stars attending, another TV appearance in the afternoon next Thursday and the way things are going, you'll be working for years to catch up with all the other bookings and the invitations that are coming in. We just need to keep riding the wave, babes, head up, no looking down or behind you. Remember that.'

'OK then, Mr Surfer Dude. We're not in Australia now you know, this is Knightsbridge.' I adopted an It-girl voice for a minute. 'And when do I get to go down under by the way? I've always wanted to do a bit of surfing on Bondi Beach.'

Jonathan chuckled. 'One continent at a time, Nat. World domination will be yours and then you can buy a beachfront house on Bondi Beach if you like. Just keep putting in the time for me for now, OK?'

'If you say so,' I said meekly.

'Is Sarah with you now? Or are you with one of the guys I keep reading about in the papers and you don't tell me about until I ask?' I heard a woman's voice in the background and Jonathan muttered a barely audible 'Thank you, just put it there'.

'Don't panic,' I said, 'I'm not going to get into any trouble. I'm all on my lonesome except for Sarah, and Steven – the stylist from the store. They've both just popped out to give me some privacy. And don't worry, I won't be seen with anyone in public that you haven't given me permission to fall in love with. God, you're like my dad!'

But I laughed light-heartedly. I didn't want Jonathan to think I was really telling him off. At the same time, I caught myself wondering what exactly I was doing giggling at stupid little comments like that, and trying not to offend anyone with my words. The old Natalie wouldn't have cared much about that. I shrugged it off with Jonathan's reply.

'You know I'll be happy for you to be happy, as long as he's good for your career, Natalie. The last thing we need right now is for you to fall for some C-lister, when you're heading towards the top of the A-list. OK, is there anything else I can do for you right now? Or shall I leave you to your shopping?'

I could always tell when conversations with JD were about to come to an end. He would ask if there was anything else I wanted and suddenly move seamlessly into businessman talk, cutting out the pleasantries. I could tell he was about to do it, but I had been wondering about something, and thought it might be a good time to ask again.

'Well, there is one thing, yeah. You know we were talking last week about me getting the camera out again and you said you might be able to get me a couple more magazine shoots? I was wondering if—'

Jonathan broke in.

'Natalie, I'll let you know if anything comes of that. We've got other fish to fry right now though. Trust me, you know I'll look after you, right?'

'Yeah, I know that. Thanks again, Jonathan. For everything . . .' I trailed off, a bit disappointed. I knew I should be grateful for what was coming my way – I owed JD so much for what he'd done for me.

'OK, then. Leave it with me. I'll let you know when

anything happens. For now though, I want you to concentrate on looking beautiful, getting yourself out there every night and getting your picture in the papers in the morning. You're the hottest girl around right now, and the press can't get enough of you. Learn to love it.'

I laughed again. He was right and I *was* starting to enjoy it. The jewellery, the flat, the clothes, the attention . . . it was a fantasy come true.

Sure, I missed my friends back home sometimes, but it was just one party after another, shopping and fun in the daytime and events and openings to go to at night. It seemed like everyone wanted to know me here and I wasn't going to ruin all that by thinking about boring old St. Albans and the sad little life I'd left behind.

'Thanks, JD. Talk to you soon.' I pressed 'End Call'.

I looked at the various reflections of myself in the full-length mirrors that covered every wall and surrounded me like an army of Natalies. I looked good, really good. The Jimmy Choos were perfect.

It was time for some serious shopping.

I called out, just above a normal speaking voice, knowing that there would be an answer immediately.

'Steven, could you get me some of these in white and another pair like this, I'll take them all.' I gave myself a moment to look around at the stacks of boxes and shoes that surrounded me and at the mirror straight ahead. I couldn't help myself. I grinned and posed, just managing to stop myself as Steven entered the room.

7

Early in November I got a call from Ravi during a photo shoot for *GQ* magazine. He left a message and during a break I happened to have some time, so I texted him back. I didn't want to talk to him while I was at work. It would have felt wrong somehow, like I was acting, trying to be the person I used to be.

He called me back later when I got back to the flat.

'Hi stranger,' he said. 'Haven't heard from you in a long time. All I know about you nowadays is from the papers I'm addicted to buying every morning.'

'I'm sorry Ravi, I really am. It's a miracle that I'm even at home now, to be honest, and I usually have to turn off my mobile when I'm out to block all the calls from the papers and stuff. And I don't really get a minute just to chill and think about things and I have missed you but it's difficult to find time and then—'

He broke in.

'Don't worry about it, Nat, I understand.' There was a pause. 'Well, I don't really understand, I can only imagine, but I understand that it's what you wanted and you've got it, so don't worry about me.'

Hearing his voice again reminded me how much I'd missed him. Ravi and I had been friends since primary school. I had been the first person he'd told when he decided to come out, the first person he'd confessed to about the cross-dressing too. I'd hidden away from him since all this started. I didn't know how to involve people from back then, or even if I wanted to.

There was another pause before Ravi spoke again. He spoke slowly, as if he was afraid of something.

'Erm, could I just ask a favour though?' Ravi wasn't usually so cautious when talking to me. I wondered if he was going to start asking me for money or something. Jonathan had warned me this might happen.

'Sure, go ahead,' I answered, unable to keep a bit of wariness out of my voice.

'Well, erm, I just wondered if you could call me back. I'm running out of credit and I've got to get some materials for art for next week's lessons.'

There was a short silence during which I managed to transport myself back into Ravi-world for a second. It wasn't an easy journey to take. Jonathan had actually advised me that I'd be better off leaving it behind completely. He said that there would be jealousy and envy, and people after me for what I'd got, not what I was, but I'd forgotten so much about the place where I had lived for eighteen years, and in such a short time. Here I was in my luxury apartment in Notting Hill and Ravi was paying for the call. I could afford to help him out with that, at least.

'Course I can, Rav, sorry mate. I didn't think. Hang up and I'll call you back.'

'Thanks, Nat, I appreciate it.'

It was almost humiliating for him. I felt terrible.

Over the next half an hour or so, we caught up with each other. Well, in reality, Ravi caught up with my life and me. He was so excited to hear about it all that I never had the chance to ask him about what he had been doing. Or that's what I told myself at least. I could have got him to talk about what was happening in St Albans, but I didn't. The truth was, I wasn't really interested.

'So what's going on? Your mum told me you'd got a place of your own. Tell me about the flat. What's the décor? Is it designer? Obviously. What equipment have you got, how much did it cost?'

I laughed. These were the kinds of conversations we used to have online. Only then it was all about a fantasy lifestyle. Where we'd live when we won the lottery, that kind of thing.

'Well yeah, I moved in about three weeks ago. I'm really sorry I haven't been in touch you know, but my feet have hardly touched the ground lately. Do you forgive me?'

There was a snort down the line. The old Ravi was returning, and I was glad to know he was still there. To be honest, I'd been starting to wonder if the whole conversation was going to be as stilted and superficial as it had been up till then.

'Princess, since when did you need my forgiveness or

approval on anything you did! What's happened to Natalie? Has she been kidnapped by Martians? I miss your mardy little comebacks, sweetie – don't you start going all ladylike and soft on me now.' There was a pause for effect, dramatic and typically Ravi. 'However, since you ask so nicely, I forgive you.'

I laughed. Part of me was enjoying this familiar banter, but things still didn't seem quite natural between us. It was as though Ravi was trying too hard to get it back to how it was, and I wasn't sure I could be bothered to make a similar effort. Not now. What was that all about?

There was some more camp, slightly hysterical laughter at the other end of the line and I joined in, a bit half-heartedly. I missed Ravi and Evie, and even hearing Rav's voice made me feel a little homesick, but that was tempered with irritation. I was too involved in my other life now, I had things to do.

'OK, you want to know what I've got. I've got a 50-inch plasma TV with hard drive and cinema surround sound. Never used it once yet, 'cos I'm never in. The flat is done out in neutrals, all chocolates and creams, two big leather sofas and a kitchen you'd love, Rav, all chrome and dark wood. Never used that either. I just get my PA to order pizzas in most of the time, unless we're going out for dinner.'

'Your PA? What the hell do you need a PA for, Nat? I thought all you did was go to parties and have your picture taken?' He laughed again, and this time I didn't even bother joining in. He was getting on my nerves. I felt bad that he was, but he was. I was going to have to wrap this conversation up soon, I thought, but I'd try and do it nicely.

'Well it's a bit more complicated than that, you silly old queen. I have to be places, be organised, and I don't have the time 'cos I've got to make sure my nails are done properly haven't I? And I've got interviews to do and my energy levels need to be right up for them or I don't come over as well as I should.' I was struggling not to sound as though I took myself too seriously. I realised how ridiculous it must all seem to him, but in reality, it was exactly how things were. Even so I decided to go for the easy option and agree with him.

'OK I admit it, it's a load of bollocks in some ways, but if you were here you'd understand. It's all a bit mad, and they tell you to focus on just yourself so that you can be as perfect as you can. It's all part of the game, Jonathan says. You're the product, and you have to be brand new every time anyone buys you. So the PA just makes life a lot easier for you to be selfish, I guess.' I examined my nails. I really was going to have say goodbye very soon, before poor old Rav got the blunt end of my mardy mood. All I wanted to do was curl up in my double-ended bath and then chat to undemanding Sarah about the plan for our evening.

'Listen Rav, there's a load more to tell, but to be honest, too much for one conversation. We'll have to get together soon. Maybe you and Evie could come down some time and I'll take you out in town.'

I knew it would never happen, but it was what he wanted

to hear. I felt like he'd been waiting for me to say it the whole time we had been talking. But I couldn't even imagine how Evie and Ravi would fit into my new life. The conversation Ravi and I were having just confirmed what I had already decided weeks ago.

There was a tiny but very definite and pointed break, before Ravi replied. I worried for a moment that I'd upset him, but if I had he was making a good job of fronting it out.

'Sounds cool, Nat . . . I'll talk to Evie. You sound happy, anyway, which is great – the main thing anyway. And I hope you're still taking pictures? You must have done loads since you started meeting all those fabulous famous people? Are you gonna take star pictures or do something else with it?'

Much as I wanted to get off the phone, I didn't want Ravi to think I'd abandoned everything I had set out to achieve when I sold those pictures to the *Sunday Newz*. But he couldn't begin to understand the pressure I was under, to be perfect, to look right, to behave in exactly the way Jonathan said I should in order to make the most of my potential.

It wasn't my pictures that people wanted from me. I understood that and Jonathan had told me really early that it would be best to wait before I took any more. I was apparently now known for the pictures taken *of* me, for my looks and my personality. I guess I was now a celebrity, someone that people liked to read about, and look at and live life through. That was my job, Jonathan told me, to make people's lives happy and to take the money I was given to do so.

'It'll happen soon, I think. Jonathan wants me to do it, but he's working on other things at the moment. It's all about timing – doing the right things at the right time, you know?' As I spoke I knew I was just spouting one of Jonathan's lines, one which I wasn't sure I believed anyway. But I was damned if I was ready to admit that to Ravi. In my heart, I knew that I wasn't like him and Evie any more. I was part of this game. This celebrity game. I was a player, if you like. And if that meant telling myself a little story for a while, then I'd do it. After all, it was going to be so worth it in the end.

8

It was the night of the new Bond premiere, and I held my first party at the flat for all the people I'd met since I'd arrived on the scene in London. It was a cocktail party, organised by Sarah, populated by models, TV stars and musicians. I hadn't much idea of what a cocktail party actually meant before Sarah suggested it, but once I'd started on the Sex on the Beaches and the Harvey Wallbangers, I began to understand the point, and it wasn't long before the party was swimming, and so was my head.

At around eight, I set off with my girls for the Odeon in Leicester Square in a black stretch limousine, provided by FHM with tinted windows. We snuggled up in the back together, sipping champagne with Sarah, Fliss from *Firefighters*, the new BBC soap opera, and DJ Smooch – the hottest new female MC – whom I'd met when we went clubbing a couple of weeks before and been inseparable from ever since. Sarah had tipped off the papers that we were going to be attending as Bond Girls past and present, and we weren't going to disappoint the photographers or the fans on the red carpet.

To be honest, the film wasn't really something I would normally be interested in. I'd always been into more unusual films, things like *Ghostworld*, *Donnie Darko* or *Lost in Translation*, but it's amazing what cocktails, followed by champagne on ice in a stretch limo, and the attention of what seemed like the entire world's press could do for a girl's interest levels in action movies. I couldn't believe the flash bulbs when we got out, although my dress, which I was told was based on Halle Berry's very revealing silver strappy dress in *Die Another Day*, certainly explained a lot.

'Over here, Nat!'

'Give us a smile, Nat.'

'Give us dirty, plenty of attitude.'

I gave them everything they wanted and more, posing and smiling, loving every minute of it, and once safely inside, we didn't stop being the centre of attention.

'What made me wear something that showed half my arse when I got out of the car?' Fliss asked, as soon as we got inside, though she was grinning like a maniac, obviously on a high from the attention. She'd just got the lead in a new West End musical about New Romantics and the eighties and never missed a chance to get some extra press.

'Shouldn't worry about it, darling,' Smooch answered. 'It'll be the biggest picture on the gossip pages tomorrow morning for sure. Who wouldn't want a piece of your gorgeous ass for their breakfast in the morning, eh?' Flashing her perfect white teeth set in an Ibiza-tanned face, she reached around and squeezed Fliss's bum gently, setting off another volley of flashes from the cameramen behind the red roped-off VIP area in which we were standing.

'I don't believe you. You'll do anything for publicity, won't you?' I laughed.

'Isn't that the pot thingy calling something something else? Or whatever the saying is?' Smooch put her head on my shoulder, her long black curls falling down over my back, and produced a pout to rival the best Posh Spice could manage. Again the flashes popped, leaving us blinded for a second. I leaned in and pouted myself, red lipstick and long brown hair framing my face for the perfect picture I knew they were seeing through their lenses.

By the time the movie was over, half the celebrities had already left. Apparently, this was how it usually worked. They would come in at the front, stay for ten minutes and then leave by the side doors in their waiting limos. We weren't quite so ready to give up the free champagne and the chance to network (under clear instructions from Jonathan, who represented all three of us) and when we left we got the biggest cheer of the night from the freezing cold crowd outside and the largest share of the pictures for the morning's papers. It was a job well done, and I reckoned that my dress had inched out the other two to get me the most attention as the sassy, sexy one of the 'new Angels'.

Afterwards we moved on to Made in Taiwan for the official party. The place was packed, wall-to-wall celebrities and waiting staff replenishing drinks before you even had a second to take a sip.

I was on a high from the crowds and the alcohol, and getting a lot of attention from guys I vaguely recognised from the soaps. I was sure one of them had been in Hollyoaks, anyway. I'd never really noticed when it had happened before. Anyway, Jonathan and Sarah had warned me about it many times, and I didn't want to mess things up for myself, so I usually kept my distance from blokes. Well, most of the time anyway. I'd had my moments, but so far managed to keep it quiet from everybody except JD and Sarah. Those two seemed to know what I was doing before I even did it.

However, a little after 1 a.m. a tired looking guy dressed all in charcoal grey walked past in the VIP area and just stopped dead right next to me. He was hardly matching the dress code we'd been given for the night, which was 'formal wear'. Most of the men in the room looked like James Bond, as had probably been the intention, black tuxedos, white shirts and black ties. This guy, along with the faded and distressed grey suit that looked like he'd bought it at Oxfam, was wearing a fashionably crumpled white shirt unbuttoned to his chest and a few wisps of dark chest hair. Normally I wouldn't have given him the time of day, but there was something familiar about him that made me look twice.

It was Jamie O'Brien, one of the singers in the boy band Mister-y that I'd loved when I was twelve. Evie and I had danced around my room many a time, jumping up and down on my bed to their album (they only made one) 'Wishing for the Stars'. We'd pretend that we were in the audience at one of their big arena gigs where there were no human beings in the audience that were male or over thirteen. I'd had posters of Jamie all over my bedroom walls. He was the dark, brooding one, and the one I'd had a major crush on. Since Mister-y had split, Jamie had hit a rough patch, so the papers had said, turned into a bit of a party animal. He tried to make it as a solo artist, but was usually too strung out on drugs and booze to really get it together. These days he was in the papers again – still living the hedonist's dream, apparently, but he was also back making music – pretty edgy, thrashy guitar stuff – a million miles from Mister-y – and record companies were finally interested again.

Jamie lingered alongside me and stared straight ahead. He looked completely out of it.

'*There's nothing that you can do that can't be done.*' I heard a whisper in my ear.

I looked sharply sideways at him. I could smell the alcohol on his breath.

'*There's nothing you can make that can't be made.*'

Maybe he was talking to himself? But the fact that he was leaning in my direction, as close to my ear as he could get without making it obvious, suggested it was for my benefit.

'*There's nothing you can say but you can learn how to play the game. It's easy.*'

He turned and looked me right in the eye.

'*It's easy*, Natalie.'

I blushed. He knew my name. Jamie O'Brien knew my name. I hadn't blushed since I caught my mum reading my diary when I was fourteen. It just wasn't something I did. But right now I could feel it spreading right down my neck and on to my chest, like a river flooding its banks. It must have matched the silver shimmer of my dress very attractively. Not.

'How do you know my name?' I managed to muster some kind of words, attempting annoyance and interest in the same question. I had suddenly become plain old Natalie from St Albans again.

'Everyone knows your name, Natalie de Silva. You're everywhere. You're on my television, in my newspaper, in my magazine . . . It would be strange if I didn't know your name, wouldn't it? Isn't that the idea? That everyone should know your name?'

Jamie held my gaze in a really unnerving way, and I couldn't tear my eyes away from his. It was like he'd locked on to me and wasn't going to let me escape. I thought I'd understood his attraction when I'd stuck his poster to my bedroom wall. I hadn't known the half of it.

'Pleased to meet you, I'm sure. I'm Jamie.'

I tried to sound composed. 'What were you say—?' But then Jamie grabbed my wrist, gently but firmly, pulling me towards him. I felt a fingernail slightly indent into my skin, before his hot breath was on my ear and my hair was burying his face.

"All You Need is Love". The Beatles. Surely even you have heard of them, Natalie?' He was sneering, but the effect was quite hypnotic. 'You should listen to them sometime. Their lyrics contain a lot of wisdom . . .'

His hand had now snaked its way round my waist, encircling the bare skin on my lower back protectively. I liked it, and wanted to see where this would lead, not sure if I was Natalie the twelve-year-old fan, or the new grown-up, glamorous Natalie. Whoever I was, Jamie O'Brien was Jamie O'Brien and I wasn't going to let this go just yet.

'I know who The Beatles were. I'm not completely cultureless you know. 1967. The Summer of Love?'

'I'm impressed. You're more than a pretty-faced little wannabe then?'

I could see the whole of Jamie's face now, the bumps and scars that populated his high, darkly shadowed cheekbones, framed by cropped, almost chopped black hair. It was his eyes that forced me to stare though. I couldn't keep my own eyes off them. They were almost too deep and dark. Like pools of chocolate.

I tried to lighten things up a little. 'You know, I was into Mister-y from the start. Me and my mate Evie bought your album when no one else had heard of you. See, I was loyal!' I laughed, but knew I must have sounded like every other groupie he'd met. 'We kind of went off you after your first solo effort, though,' I said, to redress the power balance. Maybe I was just digging a deeper hole for myself, but I suddenly felt bolder and more confident. If Evie could only see me now.

'Well I'm not sure if you weren't just missing the new levels I reached with melody and structure. At least, that's what my press release said.' He winked and took a swig from his glass, downing the contents in one. 'Perhaps I'll fulfil your very high expectations with my new album. It's coming out next month. Might even get you an advance copy, if you play your cards right.' He leaned closer. 'I'll tell you a little secret, Natalie. I knew you were a fan from one of your MTV interviews. Even if you did make a joke of the old days.' He pretended to give me a dirty look. 'Most people did. But I appreciated what you said about giving me a chance again. Some people wouldn't have done that. So thank you for that.'

I remembered that interview. I'd been asked about my musical tastes as a young teenager. If I'd known Jamie was watching me I wouldn't have opened my mouth – at least, not about Mister-y.

But he sounded so genuine that for the third time in my life I blushed. Evie was going to be squealing like a piglet when I told her about this!

Then, all at once I became aware of the room again, the lights and the noise. A space had opened up around us, and nobody was standing within ten feet of us. Beyond the dancing coloured lights in which we were bathed, I could see we had aroused plenty of interest from the other party goers, celebs, ordinary people and press alike. It was only then that

I realised I was being guided away from the rest of the party, into a more private area of the bar. Jamie certainly had his moves down.

'I don't know where my friends are. I ought to go.' I clutched my bag to my chest and tried to convince myself that I really did want to go, when I knew that that was the last thing I wanted to do. This guy had me spellbound all over again. Only this time I was an adult and in the company of some strong vodka and a slug of celebrity chutzpah in my veins. It made it all so much more rock 'n' roll.

'You know,' he said silkily, 'you're every bit as beautiful as you look in photos. Usually girls like you don't even come close in the flesh.'

I bit my lip hard, determined not to react to the back-handed compliment. This was too good to mess up with a Natalie strop.

'Maybe we could hang out for a while,' he went on. 'I've got the final demo of the album on disk down at the studio. You'd be the first person outside the record company to hear it. I think this is the big one. I'll be headlining the next Live 8 in twenty-five years on this. Want to come back with me now?'

He studied my wide-eyed expression with a smirk.

'Anyhow, it's up to you. I'm gonna get out of here soon, so you'd better make your mind up . . .'

He began to fidget, fiddling around in his pockets for something.

He was very persuasive, and so was the alcohol, but I had to play the game a little bit.

'I've only just met you. What makes you think I'm gonna go anywhere with you?'

'Because you want to know if I can do it? And you want to see if everything you've read about me is true?' He gave me a dazzling smile. 'The studio's down in Maida Vale. I've got the keys. You coming or what?' He jangled a bunch in front of me as if to prove he was telling the truth. I didn't really need the evidence. I knew I wasn't going to say no, but I wanted to make sure I said yes in the right way at least.

'OK. Maybe just for an hour or so, then.' I looked him right in the eye as I spoke, making sure he knew he hadn't forced my decision. 'And then I'm coming back to this party and home with my girls. OK?'

He nodded and smiled, running his hands through a mop of immaculately styled messy hair.

'Don't worry. Whatever you've read about me, only ninety per cent of it is true. The rest is what my publicist puts out there when it's a quiet day.'

I couldn't help laughing. He was a bit adorable. Still.

'Look, I need to tell Smooch and Sarah where I'm going, OK? And I'm not leaving with you out the front. I'll get Sarah to organise the car for the back entrance and you can meet me there in fifteen minutes.'

Jamie seemed relieved not to have to make any of the arrangements.

'You're no mug are you, Nat? Can I call you Nat? It's

what the papers call you. I don't have a watch though, so you'd better give me the signal when you're ready. Don't do watches. Don't do mugs. We make a good team.'

He beamed a slightly tainted, toothy grin and then melted off into the darkness and the milling crowd. My heart began to calm to a steady hundred miles an hour instead of the speed of light.

Evie would kill me if I didn't go. I owed it to her and all the other girls who'd loved Jamie from a distance and who would never get a chance like this. And so what if all the gossip columns were true and he'd had half the beautiful women in London? Everyone's entitled to a life, aren't they, and Jamie seemed to have turned a corner; maybe he'd even grown up at last. I smiled as I checked my hair and make-up in the VIP toilets. I was running with the pack now – and Jamie O'Brien was nothing I couldn't handle.

10

The next morning, or should I say, the next afternoon, I woke up with either my first migraine, or the worst hangover in the world. A vice was tightening on my skull, and my jaw ached. It was a matter of seconds before I was tearing out of bed and rushing to the bathroom to heave the contents of my stomach into the toilet bowl. I had no idea how much I'd drunk – or what I had or hadn't eaten. I just knew I had never felt worse. And I was pretty sure I should be somewhere doing something; I just couldn't for the life of me remember what.

I'd had a few 'interesting' dreams that night, too. Not the sort that you happily tell your friends about and then try to work out what they might mean, like I used to do with Rav and Evie. These were in a different league: there were any number of strange coincidences with people from my past joining in on events from my present, and the odd complete freak-out moment when I thought I was going to jump off things because I believed I could hover like a dragonfly. When I had finally woken up, I wasn't sure what was reality and what had been the dream.

I hoisted myself up from my seat on the bathroom floor and stumbled back to bed, where I sank my head into the fat, fluffy pillow and called Sarah on the special intercom that Jonathan had set up for us. She was only downstairs in her flat in the same complex as mine, and I wanted a strong cup of coffee and some sympathy, but she wasn't there, so I left a message.

Then I started to think.

It wasn't long before everything began to flood back.

I picked up my phone and switched it on. I'd turned it off at some point during the night, and when it started to light up and talk to me again, there were already seven missed calls and four angry texts, all from my agent.

I called Jonathan immediately.

'It's a good thing for your head that Sarah has been over here at the office today, Natalie, because if she'd been down there you would've been up a lot earlier than this. We've been calling you all day. Now what the hell do you think you've been doing?'

I suddenly felt cold. Jonathan had never talked to me like this. His tone was aggressive and distant. I'd never even heard him raise his voice before. He was clearly angry about something.

'What's the problem?' I said, my tone a lot more bolshy than I was feeling. 'I just went to the premiere with Fliss and Smooch and Sarah and then out after. Sarah must have told you that? Didn't she?'

I felt befuddled. What could have happened that

Jonathan would be so annoyed about? Slowly the cogs of my poor brain began to turn . . . We'd had a great time. I could remember the pictures, the dress, the drinks, Smooch and Fliss and . . .

. . . and Jamie O'Brien.

Shit.

Had something happened with Jamie that I couldn't recall? It wasn't an impossibility that it had, given the no-show my brain was pulling today. I retraced my steps as best I could. Jamie and I had left the party, gone back to his studio, and listened to his new album. Things were a bit hazy after that. There was definitely a bit of snogging, but nothing . . . nothing that I should be ashamed of, surely?

'I've got half of Fleet Street on my back this morning, Natalie, and they're ready to kick us where it hurts. What they've got could mean you'll never work again. Why the hell did you leave with Jamie O'Brien? Of all the people you could have chosen. You know what that scumbag is like. The whole British and European media have been trying to destroy him since he stopped being the golden boy and went around shagging everybody he could get his hands on while he was off his head on coke. It doesn't look good, Natalie, hanging round with losers like that. You're hardly Kate Moss, you know.'

It was all starting to come back to me: the secret meeting outside the back of Made in Taiwan; the ride through the West End sipping champagne in the limo; the dingy, barely lit side entrance of the little studio where Jamie had played me his music. The beat-up old sofa where we'd shared a long and lingering snog. My heart missed a beat. But surely there was no way anyone could know about that? And, anyway, big deal!

'But I don't get it, Jonathan, we only went to listen to his new album and then, well we just hung out for a bit. What have the press got? We didn't see any press the whole time. Not even when we were leaving the club.'

There was a huge, frustrated sigh at the other end of the phone. Jonathan didn't seem ready to calm down just yet, and I still couldn't work out why. Surely there wasn't anything to worry about?

'Ever heard of CCTV, Natalie? They must have that in St Albans by now?' There was a nasty, cold tone to Jonathan's voice. 'Do you remember what happened when you left the studio? About 3 a.m. it was. Well, 3.16 a.m. precisely, until 3.24. I can be precise about that, because that's what is printed in the corner of the fucking pictures I have in front of me!'

I still couldn't understand. What CCTV pictures was he talking about? Where were the cameras? And how had the press got hold of them?

'Yes, they're a little bit grainy, but I have ten still images from the CCTV camera that covers the side entrance to Sin City Studios in Maida Vale. And it's pretty clear what's going on in them.'

Suddenly it all came rushing back into my mind. The champagne on the studio sofa, the pounding, driving music and the inexplicable rekindling of my teenage crush on Jamie O'Brien, the spliffs we'd smoked, and the feeling of euphoria as we came out into the crisp night air of London: the London I was on my way to owning. I'd said I had to go, and then it had happened, as we came out of the spring-loaded security door and into the alleyway.

'They have pictures of us together?' I whispered.

'Yes, Natalie. "Together" isn't quite the word for it though, is it? In my day, there was a name for what's in these pictures, but we won't go into that right now. The simple fact is that the tabloids have ten CCTV images of you, in various stages of undress and attachment with a well-known Class-A drug addict, user and abuser of women, disgraced former pop star and general enemy of the people. It's the golden girl of the moment and the man who's gained and lost everything, in an alley behind a block of flats in Maida Vale. Hardly classy, is it? Hardly going to keep up your profile or further your career, eh? More like ruin it.'

I could barely speak. My mouth seemed glued together, and not just from the effects of emptying the previous night's excesses out of my stomach.

'Oh my God, what am I going to do? Jonathan?' My words were hardly any more than breaths. I could feel my whole world collapsing. My heart was pounding through my ribcage. This was a disaster.

'I've been stupid, really stupid. Oh my God.'

Jonathan didn't speak. It seemed that he was holding

himself back on purpose, perhaps unsure what he might say if he let it all out.

'I'm so sorry, Jonathan. Really sorry. Is there anything at all you can do to stop them printing? Anything? Please?'

I knew it sounded like I was begging.

I was.

'Well, the first thing you can do is get up, get dressed, and get back to work. You have a shoot this afternoon, and this evening you're booked for the launch of a new music TV channel out east. You need to be ready for that.'

He paused, and I felt like the end was coming. He was so abrupt, calm but almost aggressive in the way he was spitting out the words. How could it have come to this so quickly? This was going to be all over tomorrow's papers, and there was nothing anybody could do to help me now.

'By the time you've managed to sort yourself out, Sarah will be down there, and she'll explain in detail to you exactly how I've managed to save your ass this time. How we've avoided a complete meltdown in your career and given you some kind of future, for now.'

He wasn't holding anything back. I could only just begin to compute his words through the fog of my fear.

'How though, what have —?' I tried to understand what was going on.

'Don't interrupt. Just listen for a change,' he barked.

I fell silent.

'I've bought all the pictures, and all the tapes, and I've done a deal with the editors that this story will disappear.

Completely. We've paid off the studio security guy, the one who sold the pictures, and this story will never see the light of day. But I don't want you thinking for one minute that this was easy. I've been working my ass off this entire morning young lady, to save your career and your future, and I've got more to do to tie off the loose ends before this day is out. So don't you forget this. One night of stupidity has led to all of this. Your stupidity, and it stops here. You hear me?'

For a second, I felt like my heart was about to beat itself right out of my body, it was going so fast. I gulped back the wave of nausea that had overcome me and managed to squawk a few words of gratitude. I couldn't believe what had happened, or how I had been saved. I'd watched careers being destroyed from a distance when I was just a girl from St. Albans, how the tabloids built celebrities up and then ripped them apart. You never heard of them again, or if you did, they were in some sad 'where are they now' programme on Channel Five. How could I have been so stupid? I actually loved those programmes on Channel Five, but I didn't want to be in one.

One thing was for sure: I owed Jonathan big time. If he'd ridden up in shining armour on a big white horse at that moment, I wouldn't have been surprised.

The line suddenly went dead and for a few moments I stared into the autumn morning light streaming through my sheer curtains.

Everything I'd worked for could have been destroyed in a few stupid minutes. It hadn't even been that good with Jamie

O'Brien. As soon as our moment of madness, MY moment of madness, was over, he'd got out his phone and called someone, mumbling something about needing to score, and then he'd gone straight back inside the studio door without speaking to me again. I'd rearranged my clothes for a minute and then stumbled around the front of the building to where the limo was parked. He didn't even say he'd call or give me his number. The next thing I knew, I was in bed. Obviously my driver had decided to take me straight home, rather than back to the club, considering the state I was in.

I curled up into a ball, pulling the thick, snuggly quilt around me like a protective shield against the world.

11

Time passed so quickly that winter, mainly because I spent the whole time running backwards and forwards across London, trying to stick to the mad schedule Jonathan had put in place for me. There was no time to get cold, or worry about the rain, because I was never outside anyway. In the morning, I would get into the back of the car in the underground car park at my apartment complex in St John's Wood, and I wouldn't breathe in any fresh air before I returned in the evening, or the middle of the night. It was all a bit mad, but, as Jonathan often reminded me, this was no time for 'taking my foot off the gas'. It was a long way from the days when I would wander around outside for most of the weekend, taking pictures of anything and everything interesting that caught my eye. I missed that freedom, but I loved my new life more.

Christmas was coming, and I got booked for appearances at all sorts of festive events, including being asked to help switch on the main Christmas lights in Oxford Street. I had joint top billing with the boy band Love Life, and a couple of the stars from *EastEnders*. It was me who pushed the button though, and my pictures and stories that dominated the gossip pages the next day. I'm not really surprised I was all over the front and inside pages: it was a freezing December night, and the skimpy top I was wearing with no bra underneath didn't leave much to the imagination.

A few days before Christmas, I appeared on the Saturday morning kids' show, *Breakfast Club*, on CITV. It was a huge deal, lots of great exposure, and Jonathan said I should see it as a fantastic opportunity to target me more into the kids' and family market as a fashion icon and celebrity role model for young girls, while still appealing to all the students and older guys who would tune in on a Saturday morning when they were still too hungover to get out of bed.

I was just happy to be on TV.

Until now the lads' mags, tabloids and more quirky fashion magazines had been my main outlets, but Jonathan had decided I needed to go more mainstream if I was going to expand my appeal and 'stay in the public consciousness' as he put it. He didn't want me to be replaced by the next big thing, which is why I found myself in the *Breakfast Club* studios at eight o'clock on a Saturday morning in December, surrounded by thirteen-year-old girls with tinsel in their hair, and over-gelled teenage boys with too much aftershave on. I wasn't used to it, and I'd been out until 2 a.m. the previous night, but I knew it was important to get it right, so I got down to it professionally and without complaining.

My interview with one of the hosts, Matt Wilson, was scheduled for halfway through the programme, and then I was going be gunged in the yellow tank of goo that had become one of the programme's most popular moments. Matt had a blue stripe down the middle of his hair, the rest of which spiked off into every possible direction. I'd seen him out a couple of times in clubs and at parties and noticed he didn't smile all that much. In fact, he'd always seemed to deliberately ignore me in particular. He seemed a bit full of himself, considering he was just a children's television presenter with a silly haircut.

I had always thought that his too-cool-for-school attitude offscreen was because he had to smile stupidly all the time for a living, in that annoying way children's presenters do. He was grinning now, as if he had just heard he'd won the lottery and discovered the secret of eternal life at exactly the same moment.

'She was a member of the paparazzi and now she's stalked by the whole nation herself! We can't keep our eyes off her, what she's wearing, where she's going, what she has to say. So let's give a *huge* Breakfast Club welcome to fashion icon, celebrity shopper and er . . . photographer, Natalie de Silva!'

There was a big cheer from the studio audience as I walked on and sat down and it calmed some of the nerves that had been welling up inside my stomach all morning. The studio lights were hot, but I knew that the professional make-up I had on would hide anything that was less than perfect. My confidence was high.

'Thanks everybody,' I said, grinning my widest 'I'm here

and you want me' grin. 'It's great to be here. And don't think I haven't been waiting to meet you all my life, Matt.' I gave him a lopsided, pretend-shy smile, guaranteed to be suggestive without being slutty.

The kids around us sent up a huge 'whoooooooo', some of the girls giggling into their hands. The line that Jonathan had told me to use had got me started and got the kids on my side, just as he had said it would.

'Well I don't know what to say, looks like Christmas has come early for me this year!' Matt joked and pretended to be embarrassed. Then he winked conspiratorially at the audience behind him. There was a cheer and some more giggling, before he reached over to kiss my hand and laughed shyly about it afterwards.

'Matt and Nat,' he said in a stage whisper. 'We even rhyme.'

The performance was perfect. The kids lapped it up. Meanwhile Matt and I connected with cold, professional eyes that understood exactly what effect we were having and how we could milk it for all it was worth.

'So, Nat, you've had quite a year so far, darling! Everybody knows by now about how you started in the business, but our Breakfast Clubbers have always got a lot of questions and they'd love to hear about what you've been doing since. Are you ready for "The Hot Spot"?'

Some cheesy music played, and a studio assistant held up a big board that had 'CHEER' written on it. The young audience did as they were told. Matt pretended to cast a good look around for the first question.

'I think we have a question from Emily, who's from Essex. Emily? Where's Emily?'

Matt searched the group of kids sitting around our feet, and there was a brief moment of panic in his eyes.

As the camera finally focused on the girl who'd been planted – clearly not in the right place – to ask a question, Matt's grin evaporated for a moment and he swivelled around to throw an angry look in the direction of the studio director. He must be having a tantrum, I thought, about Emily not being exactly where she should have been.

Meanwhile, the first question came and I refocused myself.

'Hi Natalie. I really love the clothes you wear.' Emily was about twelve. She had too much eye make-up on and an inappropriately low-cut top over skin-tight jeans. If I was a fashion role model for pre-teens, I was a bit worried about the effect I was having. 'What's it like getting them for free all the time?'

She giggled a little and shyly held her typed card in front of her face.

'Well, Emily, first of all thanks for the compliment, it's always nice to get feedback like that . . .' I stalled, I didn't really know how to answer her question. Is it great to get free clothes? Well yeah. Doh. No that was unkind – think of something nice to say, Natalie, I told myself.

'It's great.' I tried to put some excitement into it, to give the watching audience the idea that I still got giggly about the whole thing. I managed to pull it off, without feeling it. It was hard to laugh to order. JD said it was something I needed to work on. 'I do get a lot of clothes, yeah, but sometimes I do actually pay for my own, you know.' Everyone laughed. 'And, obviously, I love shopping. But it's just that the top designers seem to want me to model their clothes for them, and what girl can resist that!'

What was I doing here? I wanted to be in bed. The kids seemed to be enjoying it though. My mind flashed with an image of Ravi sitting in his pyjamas watching this rubbish and I smiled to myself, trying to convince the audience that it was actually for their benefit.

Matt switched on his auto-grin again for a headshot to the camera.

'OK, now what about Dinesh. Where's Dinesh?' Matt pretended to look for Dinesh around the group, much more smoothly this time. The camera angle that had been set up for the boy clicked effortlessly on to our monitors. 'Ah, there he is. You have a question for Nat?'

A cute little Asian lad of about ten came into focus on the monitor and I turned slightly to face him.

'Hi Nat.' Dinesh seemed tongue-tied for a moment, so I smiled encouragingly.

'Hi Dinesh, how's it going?'

'I'm your biggest fan,' he blurted, and then stopped abruptly and looked like a startled rabbit for a moment. Then he blushed and clammed up.

'Oh thank you, that's so sweet.' I smiled again. After all,

he was a cute little kid and deserved some kind of real reaction from me. I tried to encourage him to speak by leaning towards him a little. He managed to cough out his question without looking up again.

'What's it like being a celebrity getting invited to all those parties and things?' he muttered into his chest.

'It's amazing, Dinesh. I get to meet lots of famous people and . . .' I paused for a second as I remembered that I was famous too. Sometimes I forgot that I was a celebrity as well now. '. . . and there's always something exciting to see or a new place to go. I'm very lucky.'

Dinesh nodded seriously, his thick mop of black hair flopping around madly, and came back quickly with another question. His look of discomfort suggested he'd been prompted to ask these questions.

'What do you like most about being a celebrity?'

'I think it's just the chance to meet so many people, like you guys here, and being in a position to do the things I've always only dreamed of doing,' I said, then paused, looking into the boy's eyes. 'How about you? Would you like to be a celebrity when you grow up, Dinesh?'

Dinesh's face tightened in shock as he realised he was being diverted from the script he'd been given. I felt a bit bad, but he managed to compose himself.

'No, not really. What I really want to be is a photographer like you.'

It was my turn to be startled. It seemed ages since I'd thought of myself as a photographer and for a moment I felt a harsh tug of sadness and loss. I looked at Dinesh and saw all my hopes and dreams that I'd somehow left behind. In a split second I pulled myself together and answered without giving too much away. I didn't want to dismiss his statement.

'That's brilliant. You should go for it. It's a great thing to do because—'

Matt Wilson suddenly jumped in with another, this time unscripted, question.

'The photographs were a long time ago though, eh Nat? What do you think it is about you that's made you so famous *since*?'

He gave a sly little grin that only I could detect. It probably seemed such a harmless question on the surface, to the audience and the viewers at home, but I sensed that it had been worked out beforehand, probably with the help of the director: a little bit of spice to try and make things more interesting and wind me up maybe? A way to make the presenter look better than the guest? I knew enough of the tricks of the trade by now.

'Hmm, that's a tough one really, Matt. I think it's probably all the modelling that I've done around Europe and the UK and the TV shows I've done as guest presenter and being interviewed, but I also get a lot of attention from the newspapers and television for my clothes, so to be honest, I'm not really sure. It could be all of those things.' I thought I'd answered that one pretty cleverly considering I'd often wondered myself exactly *why* I was a celebrity.

I reached my arm over the back of my chair and asked

the kids around me a general question.

'What do you think, everyone? Is it the clothes or the pictures or the TV or what?'

There were a few enthusiastic 'clothes' from the girls, and some other flattering calls about 'photography'. As I'd hoped, it came across that they thought I was famous for plenty of things, despite what Matt had been trying to suggest. I decided to drive the point home.

'And what I'm really excited about is the next few weeks. There's something very special that I can reveal as a Breakfast Club exclusive.' I stage-managed a perfect pause, as Matt, the kids and most of the crew appeared to lean in, ever so slightly. 'I've got some presenting coming up after Christmas, Matt. I've been asked to present the Brit Awards this year, and I'm also presenting a special charity concert for Children in Need at the Royal Albert Hall.'

I smiled sweetly at the kids around me, whilst Matt's face fell for a split second, his sour grapes only obvious if you looked hard enough, before regaining his professional hilarity.

'Wow! That's amazing, Nat!' he lied. 'Two of the biggest nights of the showbiz calendar! Can't wait to see it, guys, can we?'

There was a roar of approval from the audience as a stage manager to our left held up the 'CHEER' sign once again.

I smiled inwardly and prepared myself for the next part of my Breakfast Club ritual. I knew that Matt and some fat kid with a terrible haircut would enjoy grunging me and that I'd probably get twice the normal amount a guest would have to suffer, but it would all be worth it just to see him squirm again, the way he just had. It would be a long time before Matt Wilson was doing the Brits. Try never.

I turned back to receive the next question from the kids.

Jonathan would be so proud of me.

12

Things started to go wrong a couple of weeks after the *Breakfast Club* appearance, despite a really busy and productive Christmas for me in the media. I was even the *Mirror*'s 'Santa Baby' for the Christmas Eve edition.

On New Year's Eve, Smooch, Fliss and I had a night in town at London Fog for a huge celebrity charity auction. 'The Fog' was the exclusive venue for most celebrity occasions because it offered plenty of privacy, a great VIP area and opportunities for the press to get the pictures they wanted and the celebs pretended they didn't want. It was a themed do, with everyone expected to come in their best seventies outfits for the party after the auction was finished, so we spent most of the day getting ready at my flat and drinking tequila slammers from late afternoon onwards.

It had been a fab night, although, as was becoming more and more normal for me, I couldn't remember much about it by the time I staggered exhausted and drunk into my bedroom late in the morning on New Year's Day. Once I'd finally hit my lovely snuggly bed, I slept undisturbed right through that day and night and well into January 2nd. When

I'd just about recovered enough to emerge from my quilt again and take a look at the Sunday papers, I realised there was a lot more to that night than I had thought.

My picture was on the front page of my newspaper, the *Sunday Newz*, slightly to the side, but definitely part of the big 'stories' of what was probably a slow news day nonetheless. I'd been allowed a holiday from my column a couple of weeks before, which was probably just as well. The picture had me leaning at a particularly unflattering angle against a lamp-post outside the club, my dress looked all skewed and twisted around my waist, and my boobs were clearly trying to make a bid for freedom from the basque-like top half of the outfit. The worst part of it was my face. I looked like I'd been in the ring with Amir Khan for a few hours: black-rimmed eyes, my lipstick all smudged and some random ligger with his arms around me from behind, laughing with his mates as he tried to get me to stand up straight. I looked a state. A total state.

NATALIE: CHARITY CASE OR BASKET CASE?
DOES EVERY CLOUD *REALLY* HAVE DE SILVA LINING?

It was meant to be the star-spangled charity event where the celebrity world could show how much they care.

At London's premier nightclub London Fog on New Year's Eve, the beautiful people offered their support, and their cash, to the most deserving kiddies' charities in the country.

A thousand members of the glitterati paid £5000 each for the privilege of just attending, before taking part in a fabulous celebrity auction of clothes, jewellery and personal items from the lives of hundreds of stars. Everything was sold to the highest bidder and the whole, amazing starry night raised a cool two million for the lucky charities. Children First, one of the sponsoring charities, pronounced it a 'roaring success'.

Sad to say, then, that the Gossip Line has to report that everything was not as it should have been on this real 'night of a thousand stars'. More like 999 stars and one cloud with DEFINITELY no 'SILVA' lining.

There have been rumours around London these last few weeks that not everything is rosy in the garden of former *Sunday Newz* columnist Nat 'Girl Behaving Badly' de Silva. Seems the celebrity world has all turned a bit sour for our Nat. And Friday night was just confirmation of what some of us have suspected for a while now.

One very close friend describes de Silva as 'lurching from one disaster to another' and 'out of control'. This might be a surprise to some readers, but my secret sources tell me she's been a time-bomb waiting to explode, with no limits to her partying and drinking. Her wild child behaviour is of the kind we're used to seeing from Hollywood starlets and spoiled children of famous parents. Mostly it's been kept schtum, until now.

Today, the *Sunday Newz* can reveal the truth of Natalie de Silva's fall from grace.

Once upon a time, we watched the sweet girl from St Albans and her C-list mates with glee: they lit up the celebrity circuit with their down-to-earth, loveable charm.

What once seemed like 'a right laugh' to everyone watching, the energy and excitement of a star on the rise, now appears to be turning into some kind of personal disaster for the girl who came so far so fast. Maybe just TOO FAST?

DISRESPECT

On New Year's Eve I watched in horror as de Silva launched herself into this classy venue wearing little more than a couple of handkerchiefs tied with ribbon (see picture right). She had plastered herself with make-up, as had all her hangers-on, and then she embarrassed anyone who cared to notice, but mostly herself, with a series of stunts that seemed to have been set up to disrespect the charities the event represented and to draw attention away from the event to her own personal attention-seeking agenda.

Ask yourself a question, love: Can you really present for Children in Need, when all you think of is yourself? Not exactly the driven young 'role model' for all budding photographers now, eh??

See pages 3 and 4 for the truth about Natalie's Nightmare Night.

I'd never had any really bad press. There had been the odd snide comment about my dresses or things I'd said that had come out a bit wrong, but nothing like this. It came as a complete shock to me. I'd assumed that Jonathan would be able to control anything after the way he'd covered for me with the Jamie O'Brien thing, and every time I'd embarrassed myself since, I was fairly confident this would all blow over . . .

Still, once I'd read the front page, I immediately called Jonathan, then Sarah, but I went straight to voicemail both times. At first I thought maybe they were at home with their families for the holiday weekend. But after a while the real doubts set in. Were they just deliberately screening my calls? Finally I called Fliss after getting no answer from Smooch.

'Have you seen the picture of me and the lamp-post, Fliss?'

'Course I have, Nat. Everyone has. It's on the front page of the *Sunday Newz*, for God's sake. I was called for a quote yesterday by them, but I put the phone down on the guy. He was so repulsive. I spoke to Jonathan and he said to leave you to it, so I didn't call you. I didn't want to worry you. I thought Jonathan would have let you know though, or that maybe he was going to put a stop on it himself? He didn't call you either?'

'Today is the first I heard about it, Fliss. I've been in a coma since I got home from the party. How come they have all this stuff on me? I know I went a bit mad, but there's never been anything like this in the paper before after one of our big nights. Have you heard from Smooch?'

I sucked on a strand of my hair as we spoke. It was a nervous habit I had developed lately. The stylists would always tell me off, but I couldn't stop myself, even when it tasted of hairspray. Today it smelt and tasted of vomit, but that might just have been my mood.

Fliss didn't answer my question.

'Look, maybe it'll all blow over. You know what Jonathan's like. He'll sort something out. Maybe you should just lay low for a bit? Go back home? You said you'd missed the family Christmas and everything.'

She sounded concerned, but a little distant, as if she wasn't committing to something. I couldn't understand what was going on. It's not like I was a serial killer, was it?

'Look, what's the big problem, Fliss? OK, I was out of it big time, we all were. The tequila was good though, wasn't it?' I forced a laugh.

There was no response.

'But just because I wore a sexy dress and got a few more pictures than normal, everybody seems to be having a go. You're not mad with me, are you?'

There was more silence, then, 'Look, the thing is, Nat, I can't really afford to attract the sort of attention you're getting. I'm an actress, not a wannabe celebrity, and I've got a career, I need to look after my image – the production opens in three weeks. You're famous for, well . . . just being in the right place at the right time, let's be honest.' She sounded like a disapproving schoolteacher. 'Anyway, they're having a go at you for more than just the state you were in that night. Haven't you read the whole thing? It's not just the picture on the front, you know. You haven't read the stuff on the inside pages, have you?'

She sounded concerned.

I hadn't read any of the main article. I'd panicked as soon as I saw the front page and started to call around to get somebody to sort it all out for me.

'No I haven't. I'll read it now. Then maybe I can see what all this bloody fuss is about.'

There was a click. Fliss had hung up. I opened the paper again.

13

I lost presenting Children in Need at the Royal Albert Hall on the Tuesday after New Year. Within the next couple of days I'd lost the Brits as well.

Jonathan called me a couple of hours after I'd spoken to Fliss. I'd left message after message on his phone so he had no choice. He advised me, in a completely emotionless voice, to go back to St Albans for a couple of weeks and try to limit the damage. He didn't sound very reassuring, to be honest – or as if he cared that much. He told me that he'd already had some 'apoplectic' calls from a bunch of my clients saying they were 'reviewing' my contracts in crisis meetings, calling people back from their Christmas and New Year breaks. I started panicking, begged for him to help, but this time he didn't bite. It was pretty clear that it wasn't me he was worried about; it was the business he was losing because of me.

I couldn't believe that one story could change things so much, or get Jonathan so mad. When I'd actually bothered to read the inside article in the paper after speaking to Fliss, I had thought that things might be a bit difficult for a while, but I should have known better, given how I got started in this backstabbing world of celeb hell.

Apart from the drunken fall outside the club, there were 'eye witness' accounts of my 'disgusting behaviour' from a variety of sources. They had printed a detailed, but anonymous, explanation of how my 'embarrassing clash' with a former *Big Brother* contestant had exploded into life. Apparently it had ended when I had thrown a drink in her face and called her a 'F**cking Wh*re Wannabe', as the newspaper and 'sources close to the discredited de Silva' coyly put it. This was, apparently, because she had 'moved in' on somebody I was 'trying to bed'. I did vaguely remember some kind of small disagreement about the seating plan and an amicable conclusion to it between me and the woman in question, but maybe I was wrong? There were also video images of my various 'celebrity tantrums', caught on a mobile phone, available for download on the paper's website, so maybe I'd lost my memory after all? I didn't visit to check.

There were also colour pictures of my 'full-on lesbian clinch' with Smooch, which had happened during a particularly intense part of the celebrity auction event. J-Lo had donated a bikini from one of her early videos, by way of Elton John, and the bidding was climbing way above expectations when the attention of the bidders had been 'deliberately seized by Natalie de Silva, who forced herself on her friend DJ Smooch in some bizarre girl-on-girl frenzy' at their table. Not only was it 'totally without class', it had caused such a stir as to interrupt the bidding. Only the intervention of Bozo, lead singer of veteran rockers W7, managed to save the day. The reporter noted that to many of those present, the incident seemed to be a 'calculated plan to draw attention to Natalie de Silva and away from the event itself. It was nothing but a cheap publicity stunt.' I just remembered it as a stupid kiss when Smooch had dared me to do it, but even I had to admit, the pictures did look bad.

Each photograph was accompanied by direct quotes from that same so-called mate Smooch, in which she said she had been shocked by my behaviour and wanted me to apologise to her and the charities, because all she'd wanted from the evening was to 'give a little back to the kids, not be part of some freak show'. She couldn't understand why I'd started to completely lose the plot, and felt I was 'on a slippery slope' and if I wasn't careful everyone that used to care for me would disown me.

Smooch did go on to vow to try and help me, if I 'could be helped now', for which I was, of course, extremely grateful, having read it in a national newspaper and not having heard it from Smooch in person . . .

I hadn't been aware until that moment that I was on that much of a slippery slope, but all of a sudden it seemed like there were plenty of people out to push me down one. And quickly. I hadn't bargained for this. I just thought I'd been having a good time, living it a bit large. What a naïve fool.

Most damaging of all was the main report from the article. Above a picture showing me about to climb into a car as I left the venue, the headline screamed:

JUDAS WITH DE SILVA

Over my shoulder was the free Prada goodie bag containing £4000 worth of sponsored gifts that every celebrity had been given in return for their attendance, along with, under my other arm, a huge cheap stuffed teddy bear wearing a T-shirt with the logo of one of the prominent children's charities for which the evening had been a benefit.

Unfortunately, what completely detracted from my positive support for the kiddies' charity was the fact that with my free hand, I had my middle finger stuck up straight and proud, as I aggressively threw a defiant face right at the camera. It looked for all the world like I was walking out of this charitable auction evening and party with my free goodie bag, my free stuffed bear, no purchased auctioned items at all and a particularly bad attitude towards the event and the charities it had all been done for.

I myself knew that the picture had actually been taken seconds after I'd deliberately been shoved against that rusty old lamp-post – right into the greasy hands of some liggers outside the nightclub. Of course, the picture told a different story because the nice paparazzi man had engineered the whole thing, and that middle finger I'm giving? That was directed at him.

Only that bit wasn't mentioned in the article.

14

Mum phoned the following weekend, the first friendly voice I'd heard for days. We hadn't spoken since Christmas Day, and even then it had been Mum leaving a message on my answerphone at the flat because I'd been over at JD's house for a business gathering/party. My grandma had wished me a Merry Christmas and a Happy New Year, too. I'd laughed when I heard it – not really bothered. But now it made me feel just a little bit empty.

Yep, things were very different now, which is why I nearly burst into sobs when I heard Mum's voice.

'Natalie love, we've all missed you so much, you know. I saw Ravi in the precinct the other day, and he was saying he'd love to hear from you. That was before all this happened with the papers and everything, and I'm sure he'd like to help. Come home, love.'

I put a brave front on. 'Mum, I've got so much going on down here. I need to be around so I can sort things out. It's a bit of a mess. Jonathan wouldn't want me to run away from it all.'

I expected complete surrender once Jonathan was

mentioned. They'd basically left everything to him from the minute I left for London. Nothing had happened in the past to make me expect anything less than full co-operation with his wishes. And anyway, Kathleen de Silva wasn't shaped from the same mould as me. She had always been prepared to give in to her darling daughter and JD, when either of us put her under the slightest pressure.

'Well, actually love, Jonathan called us last night and said it would be much better if you were at home for a couple of weeks. He said you were under a lot of strain right now, and that some time away would give you a break . . .'

She trailed off. There was a pause. Jonathan had called my parents?

'He's sending a car around for you at about half past four, to your flat. I think you should take his advice you know. He always seems to know best. At least, he has done so far. And in a way, love, you've only got yourself to blame for what's gone wrong now.'

Mum's voice had an unexpected firmness to it. Or maybe it was just that I wanted to hear it, so I did. In any case, something inside me crumpled for a moment, and I gave in. Maybe she was right, and it was all my fault, although I still had trouble understanding the horrible way I'd been treated in the media considering what I'd actually done. But the way things were at the moment, with the washing-up piling up in the sink and the pizza boxes starting to gather around the bin, the thought of not having to be in control of my whole life and destiny for a bit was quite appealing. What could I lose by giving myself some breathing space? In a couple of weeks I would be back in London and things would be OK and back to normal.

'All right. I'll come back for a bit. You're right. I need to get some things sorted and I could use the break. It was a busy Christmas.'

Mum spoke for a couple more minutes, but I didn't hear much of what she said. I was thinking about going home, and being the old Natalie again. I'd protected myself from home for months now, making sure I had the least amount of contact that I could with my past life and everything it represented. That was failure. This was success. I had been so desperate for London to be my reality that I'd blocked St Albans out completely. Now I'd have to find out if there was still some part of me there and how much of St Albans was still in me.

I came back to the present as my mum finished the call with a sentence I hadn't heard from anyone for a while. 'And bring your washing back home with you, love. I'll get it done properly for you.'

Despite the dark cloud above me, I couldn't help a weak smile at that. I could just see Kathleen de Silva trying to wash and rinse out my latest Dolce and Gabbana tops and my La Perla lingerie.

It would be good to be home again. If only for a very short visit.

15

I spent the first evening back in St Albans trying to avoid telling my parents exactly what kind of life I was really leading in London, as if they didn't know already. We sat around the tiny dining table in the kitchen on Bletchley Street, and for much of the time didn't have much to say after I'd been updated on Grandma's latest health scare and the shocking cost of houses in the St Albans area now. Once I'd blocked a couple of questions about me and my life, they seemed to decide it wasn't worth asking, and moved on to a counselling approach instead.

They were really concerned, which was lovely, but after a while I just felt incredibly tired, more tired than I'd ever felt in my life before. It was as if I had been living on one of those beds of nails for six months; the points had been pricking into every little part of my body, forcing me to be alive and stay awake, no matter how much it hurt. Finally, I made my way slowly up the old stairs, my designer sandals padding on the carpet I'd bumped down on my bottom when I was a tiny little girl, and crashed into the bed linen that smelled of home, family and my mum and dad's love.

It was late afternoon when I woke up, and there were noises outside. I peered around the curtains to see the familiar sight of a group of male photographers, smoking cigarettes and talking guardedly into their mobiles. It felt like life had come full circle since the end of the summer and I was back to square one. I felt rested, but sensed the hunted feeling starting to come back again. I knew I needed to escape.

I called Ravi and Evie, and we arranged to take a trip back in time, to our favourite pub, the one we'd been going to ever since Evie had passed her test, out in the country and away from prying eyes. We'd shared stories of Ravi's love life, or lack of it, there, solved all sorts of complications and problems of our own. It was where we'd all dreamed of making it: me as a photographer, Ravi on reality TV, Evie as an international hotshot lawyer.

By hopping over the back fence of our little garden and down the side dirt road that separated our house from the rest of the close, I was able to make my getaway and into the back seat of Evie's little Nissan Micra.

Once we got to the Rose and Crown I began to relax. I'd spent most of the journey hiding under an old picnic blanket I'd asked Evie to bring along for me, and half expected a car to come tearing around a bend behind us, or some motorbike to draw alongside and stick a camera in my tartan-blanket-covered face. I'd forgotten what it was like to sit in a car and not be stared at. I'd also forgotten how small normal people's cars were in the back. By the time I relaxed for the last few moments of the journey, my legs were killing me from being curled up behind the driver's seat for half an hour.

Even at the pub I was still a bit antsy, but once I realised that no one was actually looking at us in our section, I felt better. There was hardly anybody there anyway. It was that funny time between afternoon and evening when nobody goes into pubs except the really local locals, or people with something to hide.

'Here you go, a packet of salt and vinegar and a Vodka Kick. I don't think they do tequila slammers here.' Ravi chuckled to himself as he sat down, until he realised I wasn't laughing at all. Then I punched him hard on his shoulder.

'Knob.'

'Yes please, if you're offering.' He laughed again. This time we all did, although without any real humour behind our laughter. Ravi and Evie seemed to need my permission to react to anything, like they were waiting for me to give them the rules of our new situation.

'You're not telling me you haven't been overrun with admirers the past six months, Rav?' I tried to inject some old-style sarcasm into the atmosphere, to lighten the mood.

'Chance would be a fine thing, princess. Anyway, can you imagine me walking down the high street holding hands with whoever in the pedestrian precinct and then running into my uncle walking the other way? Or my dad? Holy shit! I'd rather be single and entertain myself in my bedroom.'

He drew his breath in sharply.

'Eww, enough of the details already thanks, Rav.' Evie covered her face with both hands in mock horror at the thought of Ravi's night-time behaviour.

I looked at his beautiful smooth, light bronze skin and deep brown eyes. In London he would be all right. Everyone would fancy Ravi. Even the straight boys.

'You're in the wrong place at the wrong time, mate,' I said. 'You need to get yourself out of this place. You both do.'

Evie and Ravi's eyes met for a brief moment. I sensed some tension but it seemed to disappear as quickly as it came. Maybe I was only being paranoid again. Jonathan had told me that I was prone to paranoia just the other day.

'Well, yeah, obviously Nat, we do realise that. But it's not like we're not trying.' Evie did sound a little bit annoyed. 'We're both going to Uni next year. So we'll be out of here then. Not everybody is as lucky as you were, you know.'

I'd completely forgotten that this was their last year at college; I'd been so wrapped up in my own world. I felt a bit guilty, but not that much. It wasn't my fault they had been stuck here and I was living it up in London. You make your own luck in this world. And anyway, what did they expect, especially Evie? She was still wearing the same jeans she'd bought from TK Maxx two summers ago. Even then I'd told her she was sad and now, looking at her and Ravi in turn and seeing their defeated expressions, I couldn't get it out of my mind that they hadn't moved on even the slightest bit since I'd left.

'Oh yeah, of course. So where are you off to?' I tried to sound enthusiastic. It was a trick I'd learned at endless photo shoots.

'I'm going to Leeds hopefully, if I get my grades. Evie's already got in at Cambridge to do Law.'

This time I enveloped Evie in a genuine hug. 'Cambridge! Ev, that's fantastic, I'm so proud of you!' It was the truth, I was really chuffed for her. I could see I didn't really need to worry about her getting stuck in a rut. Talking of which, I turned to Ravi.

'Whooo, Leeds eh? Centre of the known universe!'

I laughed at my own joke.

Ravi didn't.

'Yeah, Leeds. It's the best place in the country for my course. And you know I've always wanted to go there.' He glowered into his drink.

'Well, I suppose there must be more of a gay scene up there than in St Albans, right?'

I flicked my hair out of my face. I was conscious that it hadn't been styled for over a week now. I was trying really hard here to connect, but nobody was throwing me a lifeline.

'Yeah I suppose. That's not all that matters to me, though, is it?' Ravi didn't look at me. In fact he looked like he was concentrating on not looking at me.

'What about you then?' He seemed to speak through gritted teeth. 'You would have been going to Uni this year too. Are you even a bit bothered?'

From Ravi's expression I could tell he had already

decided what my answer would be. There was a mixture of envy and pity. It was something I was already starting to get used to.

'Not bothered really, no. I mean, I haven't done any photography for a while and I kind of miss it, but there's never any time for it anyway. I sometimes think, like, "Ooh, I should take some pictures at the weekend some time", but then there's the press outside the front door and there's no peace and quiet, and how am I supposed to take pictures if there are twenty fat blokes in the way?'

They both smiled lamely. And the thing was, I was lying. I still wanted what I'd always wanted. But things had got so out of control. I couldn't see how I was going to get things back on track now. It was better to front it out to Ev and Ravi, though.

'It's not easy, you know. Sometimes I even wish I was still here, doing my A-levels and taking photographs whenever I like.' Looking at the table, I realised I hadn't touched my drink and neither had anyone else. There was an uncomfortable silence for a moment or two.

Evie pressed on, seeming to seize an opportunity she'd been waiting for.

'So what if you did that *now* then? I mean, you're not going to be doing the other stuff as much, at least for a bit. So you could just get on with your own thing again. Like you used to do, remember? Like we all did.'

She was such a romantic. Maybe it was the wild hair and her passionate eyes, but I always felt Evie had been born in the wrong decade, maybe even the wrong century. She was like something out of a Brontë novel at times.

'Evie, think about it. As if I could ever come back here. It would be hell for me. Can't you see that?' I was annoyed that she could even suggest such a thing to me. 'Yeah, I could try. But why would I? In a few weeks, Jonathan says people will have got over the New Year's Eve thing and then things will be back to normal in London. And anyway, St. Albans is such a shit hole. You know it is.'

'Yeah, well maybe,' Evie replied. 'But don't you think you're going a bit over the top, Nat? I mean, the drinking every night and falling out of clubs, all that lesbian stuff during the auction, giving the finger? Do you actually think there's a way back from all that? The papers are having a right go at you every day at the moment. You're definitely not their flavour of the month any more.'

Evie could stick the knife in when she wanted to. I'd forgotten that. I'd thought I could get away from people who judged me if I came here. Wrong.

'I'm aware of that, Evie, you don't need to go on about it. What about you, Ravi? Do you agree with Evie? Should I come back to St Albans and try and be what Evie thinks I should be?' I challenged.

Ravi looked down at the table as he spoke.

'I think you could maybe wait around here for a few months and then try and go back. It's not going to be easy. But I do agree with Evie, yeah.'

Ravi looked at me defiantly. I stared at them both in

horror. This was the guy who had made a video of himself naked, eating Chicken Vindaloo out of his belly button whilst singing 'YMCA' by the Village People, in his third failed attempt to get himself on to *Big Brother*. And now he wanted me to give up on my chance to make it?

'I . . . I don't even know what to say. You just don't get it, either of you, do you? You just think it's as easy as that. One, two, three, and everything changes back to what it was. You're mental, both of you'.

I leaned back in my chair and picked up my handbag.

'Could you just take me home please, Evie? I think it would be better if I went now.'

Just at that moment we were interrupted. An old man with a pair of dirty wellies and big white whiskers had ambled over from the bar. He was a regular and I remembered seeing him many times before on our previous nights out here; part of the furniture, but always with a kind word for anyone who stood next to him as he sat on his own personal stool at the bar. I wondered if he wanted a contribution to the village church roof collection or something.

'Are you Natalie de Silva?' he asked sharply, ignoring the fact that we were clearly in the middle of a difficult and tense situation ourselves.

'I am, yes. Why?' I was shocked at being recognised in a place like this, especially by someone so old, and at that particular moment. I had thought we were safe from any unwanted attention, but still, I wasn't worried about him. Why would I be worried?

'You should be bloody well ashamed of yourself, girl. Some people around here used to say that we ought to be proud of you for making something of yourself. But you're nothing but a common tart, are you?'

Ravi rose a little in his chair and began, 'Now wait a minute, mate . . .'

'You want to get back to London where you belong and don't come back here. We're decent round here. Not like you. You're not welcome.'

There was so much spite in his words that I couldn't speak. He looked like everyone's favourite grandad: snowy white hair and a lined face crinkled up like leather and a slightly worn working suit that matched his age perfectly. If I'd seen him on the street a year ago, I would've made sure I smiled, just to make him think the younger generation weren't all so bad after all. I used to do that sort of thing a lot. Being different had been important to me.

Now the reality of my situation hit me. If people like that, good people who genuinely tried to see the best in others, had turned on me, what chance did I have?

'I really don't know what . . .' I mumbled half-heartedly.

'Oh, clear off, you little tart.' the old man said coldly.

I looked up to see the landlord standing watching us from behind his bar. He was younger, perhaps in his thirties, but he didn't step in to help. In fact it looked like he'd have been happy to join in.

Ravi looked from one to the other, open-mouthed.

'We were just going anyway,' he said. 'Come on, Nat, we'll drop you home.'

Ravi and Evie waited protectively in the room until I'd walked past the men at the bar, who stared intently at me as I passed. I felt their eyes burn into my neck as I walked out into the freezing winter air outside.

On the ride home, nobody said a word.

I knew one thing for sure. I was truly alone. The only person who could help me now was Jonathan, and I needed him more than ever.

16

It was a week later that my world finally collapsed around me.

I'd tried to relax, spend time with my mum and dad, watch TV and hang out at my grandma's. But all the time I had been waiting for Jonathan to return my many calls, checking my mobile every two minutes, desperate for any kind of contact from him so that he could tell me everything would be all right. His number rang, but he never answered. I was going out of my mind.

The stories in the papers were diminishing in length and nastiness every day, and I did try to take that as a good sign. On the other hand, the fact that I was no longer in the news worried me too. I'd never had a day without press, whether it was good or bad press, since the day the original photographs had been published last September. What if things were moving on without me and my moment had really passed – my so-called fifteen minutes of fame was up? Was I already a has-been at the age of eighteen?

In the end Jonathan contacted me twice on the same day, once by email, followed by a phone call, obviously made when his assistant told him that she'd got the 'read receipt' which confirmed that I'd opened and read his email.

By the time he called I was practically hysterical.

The email was icy and business-like.

Natalie,

I hope you're well.

Clearly the scope of our business relationship has been greatly reduced, if not hindered, recently and that has affected all of us. I do not know if you are aware of how difficult the situation has been, but it does seem that it will be very hard for us to turn matters around to our satisfaction. None of the companies to whom you are contracted are prepared to honour those contracts, because you have broken the terms and conditions applied to them. You did this by bringing products and companies into disrepute as a result of your inappropriate behaviour over a significant period of time and in particular, in one major incident.

In addition, there are problems with your account with Jonathan Davies Associates. Over the past six months we have bankrolled you for your accommodation and lifestyle (Personal Assistant, communication, travel costs etc), in addition to providing top-level publicity *services for you as our client. I am sure that you know how successful we have been in providing you with a level of status and celebrity that has enabled you to develop your career beyond that which you might have expected.*

However, I would like you to look closely at the attached document, which clearly states your very unfortunate financial situation and that you now owe this company a significant sum of money. As a matter of urgency, you need to consider strategies for repayment of these debts and how you might satisfy our demands for those repayments within the allotted timescale.

Your situation comes as a result of the aforesaid sudden and highly regrettable downturn in your fortunes, and the need for this company to take action to protect our investments and ourselves by immediately claiming back the costs of this venture, costs that we advanced to you against your future income.

Please specifically note the information regarding:

- *Cancelled contracts*
- *Cancelled income from future royalties*
- *Significant penalty clauses that you now*

incur under the terms and conditions of those contracts
- *Your living expenses and accommodation costs deducted from past earnings*
- *Our expenses for services rendered*
- *Our charges for services rendered.*

Jonathan will contact you in the next hour with a view to discussing the exit clauses in your contract with this company.

Yours,
Julianne Bracewell
PA to Jonathan Davies

When I downloaded the financial breakdown I was devastated. According to the figures, which I wasn't in any position to disagree with, having left the money side of things completely to Jonathan, I now owed Jonathan Davies Associates the sum of £73,000.

And I had no savings to my name, anywhere. I had believed that my income was already enough to set me up for life. How wrong could you be?

Jonathan called exactly one hour after I'd read the email and I began to wonder if he was taking some sort of weird pleasure in making me suffer. I couldn't understand how he had changed so much, so quickly. I'd trusted him completely, right from the start, and just because of a few drinks too many and a very unfortunate photograph, he was turning on me. It almost felt like, all of a sudden, he was out to destroy me.

I lay curled up on my bed in my St Albans bedroom, staring at the ceiling tiles that had greeted me on so many mornings as I was coming round to reality after a soft and safe night's sleep. Today felt anything but safe. Holding the phone in my hand, it felt like the room was closing in on me.

'Yeah Nat, well, business is business you know. I can't carry you at the levels you've been spending, not now things have gone down the dunny, so to speak.'

I could hear splashing and laughter in the background at the other end of the phone. My house was silent, my parents both out at work, thank God.

'But it's not like this will be forever, Jonathan. I know I've been stupid, but I can get back to where I was. Can't I go in the papers or on TV and say sorry and do some really high-profile charity work or something like that? You know how much I've got to offer and what we can do together. You always said we made a great team . . .'

I was gabbling desperately. I needed his advice. But more than that, I wanted some sense that he cared, that he was still prepared to look out for me.

'I've looked into all of it, Natalie, but nobody's biting. It seems you really have put a lot of people off with your antics. The Jamie O'Brien thing didn't help. The editors were waiting for you to fall flat on your face again after that, and they were happy to see you put it right there in their laps for them. I'm afraid they see you as soiled goods, my love. They weren't going to listen to me a second time when I tried to bail you out. Just a sec—'

I heard the clink of a glass and another ripple of water.

'Excuse me, Natalie, just getting a cocktail. It's beautiful down here at the villa today. Awesome heat for this time of year. The pool is the perfect cooler.'

I imagined Jonathan sitting in his swimming pool in Marbella with his cocktail glass, Bluetooth device strapped to one ear and a bunch of pretty girls lounging on recliners nearby. It was the sort of picture he had all over his office, demonstrating to anyone who visited just how great it was to be rich and powerful. He'd told me many times that he'd invite me down there when things started to calm down a bit and I had some time off to chill.

Fat chance I'd get to see the villa now. But that was the least of my worries. He continued.

'I did tell you, that you mustn't fuck up a second time, didn't I? It's not like I didn't warn you. Anyway, you need to put it all out of your mind now and think hard about this money you owe us.'

I interrupted, scared of what he was saying.

'Please, Jonathan,' I pleaded. 'You have to help me sort this out. There must be some way to get me back into the papers and get the contracts sorted out again? I haven't got any money to pay you back anyway.'

'Natalie, Natalie. There are new people out there now for the paps to get their teeth into. New faces, new brands.

You're old news, I'm afraid love. It's what this business is all about.' He paused, for effect it seemed. 'You shouldn't get too down, though, just think about what a great experience it's all been. Something to tell the grandchildren back in St. Albans.'

He actually laughed as he said it.

It seemed like minutes before I could speak, and Jonathan didn't seem to want to help me out by offering me any kind of hope now.

'Jonathan, please, I'm begging you. I don't have any money, let alone what you say that I owe you. How am I ever going to pay you back?'

I tried to focus on some of my framed photographs that lined the walls of my room, alongside posters of various indie bands. I avoided the Jamie O'Brien, Citizen Sheep gig flyer that was wedged into the edge of one of the frames, as I felt the beginnings of some tears pricking my eyes. I couldn't remember the last time I'd cried and I'd vowed that I never would again. I didn't know if I could hold on to that promise right now.

'I'll do anything. Anything at all to get it all back.' I needed his help. Surely he would help?

'Anything Nat? Be careful what you wish for, princess.' There was a jagged, smarmy laugh on the other end of the line. I was beginning to feel hatred for this man who held my whole life and future in his hands and no longer seemed to care what he did with it.

'Within reason, Jonathan,' I mumbled through my

humiliation. 'Is there anything at all you can think of that I could do?'

In Spain, the sun was shining down on Jonathan Davies and his associates. In St Albans there was a chill in the air but no chance of snow. That would've been too pretty on a day like this. I couldn't expect anything but ice.

'I'll see what I can do, Natalie. Don't hold your breath, but I'll make some more enquiries. If you're telling me the truth, and you're willing to do anything, then there might just be some leads I can follow. I'll call you later today if I've got anything for you. Meantime, you'd better break open your piggy bank, darling, and start counting your coppers.'

The line went dead. I dropped my mobile on the bed, turned on my side and stared at the black hole of my future until the tears started to come.

17

We all met in a back-street, old-time coffee place near King's Cross Station called Guiseppe's. It wasn't easy to find, and when I arrived I could see why JD had chosen it. The windows were completely steamed up, and the only people in there looked like they had been there all their lives, as extras to the movie called 'Life' that was taking place outside. It was the perfect place for a famous, or maybe infamous, person to have a secret rendezvous.

Jonathan had told me he had a plan, the day after our conversation about my financial situation, whilst refusing to actually tell me anything specific about what it might involve. He'd left me hanging for twenty-four hours, the perfect length of time for me to start to lose all sense of hope that he could still help me, and to begin to stare the disaster of my ruined future right in the face.

By the time he called, I'd already shared a little bit of my predicament with my mum and dad, who were obviously totally horrified, and they had started to plan for the moment when they would have to bail me out, losing the home they'd lived in all their lives in the process and generally becoming bankrupt to save me. Dad had been particularly brutal about Jonathan.

'That man is an absolute scumbag.'

This amounted to severe verbal abuse for my mild-mannered father.

'There should be a commission somewhere to complain to about these people and their behaviour. To do this to a young girl fresh out of school is simply abominable.' His outrage was comforting, if not particularly helpful at that moment, and it was a perfect de Silva moment of denial, meaning that, as usual, they didn't put any of the blame on to me for the situation, at least not while I was still in the room.

But there was a chink of light in the darkness. Jonathan wasn't going to let me down – at least I prayed he wouldn't.

Jonathan's call had been particularly mysterious and he'd refused to answer any questions. He simply gave me some veiled hints that I might be able to take photographs again, a set of instructions for how to get to the coffee bar, a date and a time which was two days away and a description of a man in his early thirties who I should look out for, should Jonathan arrive at Guiseppe's later than we did.

As it was, I was the last to arrive. I figured that I was the only one who had travelled by Network Rail.

'Ah Natalie, how are you my darling? You look wonderful, as ever.' Jonathan beamed as I reached the table they had chosen in the dingy corner next to the counter. Hidden as I was by a high-collared overcoat and tight woolly hat my mum had made me wear to escape attention on the Thameslink train from St Albans, I was surprised he could even recognise that it was me.

Even though I couldn't imagine anything worse than a warm, luvvy embrace from my publicist, I got one, with a kiss on each cheek for extras and I really didn't have much choice in the matter. But if I had to suck it up right now then I would. I needed him too much to make a big deal out of resisting his over-the-top welcome. In addition, the effect of Jonathan jumping up to give me the bear hug was enough to prevent me from being able to see anything of the other person that was sitting at the table.

Once I'd been introduced, I could see that this must have been a deliberate plan of his. Getting me seated without seeing the guy meant it would be just that bit harder for me to make a scene and leave when I saw who the mystery person was.

'Natalie, I'd like to introduce you to one of the finest photographers of his, or any generation: Marcus Raymont. I'm sure you'll be acquainted with his work.'

Jonathan made it sound like we were at the National Portrait Gallery, meeting the creator of the finest exhibit. My indulgent smile of greeting, practised over many months of celebrity schmoozing, froze as I heard the name and saw the face at the exact same moment: Marcus Raymont? Holy Shit. Now I could understand why Jonathan had made such a mystery of this. He knew most people wouldn't want to be within a hundred yards of this man, let alone at the same table in a coffee house.

'Umm, hello.' I fumbled for some words that didn't convey what I was really thinking. This was something altogether different to what I'd expected. Marcus Raymont, of all people. However, I had to take something from this meeting. I was desperate. My hand went out limply to meet that of one of the most hated men in England. There was no way that this guy would be getting any air kisses or fake hugs from me.

Raymont grasped my hand gently and began to draw it to his lips. I pulled it away before it got there, trying not to draw attention to the snub.

'Hello to you too, Natalie. Lovely to meet you. I've read a lot about you.' The voice came from inside a swirl of scarf and hoodie around his head and shoulders, designed in exactly the same way as mine: to avoid detection by the public and press on the London streets.

The thing was, in spite of all my many problems, I knew that Marcus Raymont's need for anonymity was far greater than mine.

'Great, great.' Jonathan beamed again between Raymont and myself before switching, in an instant, to a face of serious intent. 'Now, let's get down to business before we all start falling in love with each other, right?' He leaned back over his chair and called to an ancient, leathery looking man behind the counter. 'Guiseppe? Three lattes over here, mate. With the usual trimmings!'

I caught Marcus Raymont looking at me out of the

corner of my eye. Behind the cool, there was a glint of intrigue in his eyes, set in a tanned and, for someone in his forties, fresh looking face.

'Now then. I'm pretty sure you two know everything there is to know about each other, given the amount of publicity there's been about you these last few years, so let's not beat about the bush. Natalie, I'm offering you the chance to get back to what you do so well, and what got you into the business in the first place. You're a good photographer and you have an eye for the money shot. You've proved that. I want you to take pictures again, with Marcus.'

Both Raymont and I seemed to hit the button marked 'Incredulous' at the same moment.

Before either of us could respond, Jonathan ploughed on. He turned his attention to Raymont, who held his gaze with a piercing glare. There was something almost royal about him, the way he was looking down his nose at us, or particularly, me. I could tell his clothes were expensive. He was traditionally attired in a Savile Row suit, like he thought he was some sort of James Bond. Austin Powers, more like, I thought uncharitably.

'Marcus, you have all the connections in the world, but you need a partner, someone who can help you to expose the filth and degradation of this celebrity circus we live in and the press who perpetuate it, someone you can hide behind in case the world discovers you're back. Natalie's your girl. She's young, she's beautiful, she takes a good picture, but most of all, she's got it all to prove and she's hungry to make a living.'

Jonathan had barely blinked, or taken a breath. He turned back to me and took hold of both of our hands.

'I want the two of you to get your own back on the people who have punished you for those little 'indiscretions' that have got you to where you are today.'

He nodded at the steam running down the windows and the shabby tablecloth beneath our joined hands and continued. 'The press, the celebrity who stopped returning your calls, the people who accused you of being in league with the devil, the friends you thought you had who suddenly disappeared into the night. It's time for revenge, guys.'

I hadn't a clue what was going on, though he obviously had a plan. But from where I was sitting, as long as it involved money and the chance to dig myself out of the hole I was in, I'd do it. It had to be way better than my dad's best attempts. But to work with Marcus Raymont?

'You need each other, my friends,' Jonathan continued. 'It's time for you to take on the world again, and if I know you two, the world won't stand a chance.' He laughed.

There was a moment's pause as Raymont and I looked at each other again in silence.

Abruptly, Jonathan dropped our hands to the table and reached into his inside jacket pocket.

'And now I'm going to leave you with this envelope. I'm afraid I've got to be somewhere else right now, although I'd love to spend more time watching you two get to know each other. So, if you want to go along with what's inside it, let me know. If not, I'm sure we'll have other things to discuss. Although certainly nothing as lucrative for either of you, by any means.'

He looked at me pointedly.

'Jonathan, what the—?' I tried to interrupt.

'Just read what's in the envelope, Natalie. Do as you're told, and everything in your world will be hunky dory again. Trust me.'

Jonathan laid a chubby hand on mine again, pressing it damply against the red plastic of the tablecloth.

'And it's not as if you're really in a position to say no, is it, darling?'

He winked.

In a second, he was gone, just as the lattes arrived on the table, leaving me staring into Raymont's piercing blue eyes.

Jonathan didn't even leave the money to pay for the coffees at his own meeting. Yet another brilliant piece of business, no doubt, in the mind of my publicist.

Although just at that moment, alone and faced with the repulsive 'Killer Pap' as the media had labelled him, Jonathan's lack of integrity was the least of my worries.

18

'Well, are you going to open it up, or shall I? I always think "Ladies First" is the correct etiquette in these situations, but I imagine that a girl like you would like to abandon such pretensions and let me get straight to it. Am I right?'

I could see what Raymont was trying to suggest, but I wasn't going to let him get to me. I needed whatever was in that envelope too badly for that.

I grabbed it from the table and ripped open the flap.

Quickly, I scanned the contents, groaning inwardly, and tossed the card on to the table next to Raymont's still full latte mug.

'It's all yours.'

Raymont's long, bony fingers reached slowly for the card.

Marcus and Natalie
Raymont and de Silva for the Davies Photographic Agency.

Has a lovely ring to it, don't you think?

The Assignment:

You are to work in partnership with each other, under my leadership, in a new enterprise of mine. You will be contracted to work exclusively for Jonathan Davies Associates as my personal photographers.

For every story I have to sell, for every client I need to support with evidence, or every individual that my client wants me to discredit with evidence, for every opponent I need to consign to defeat, you will provide that evidence.

I know you both and I know that you will take any measures necessary to achieve what I ask of you. Obviously, I would not want you to do anything against the laws of whatever country you happen to be working in, but I trust that the two of you, of all people, will get the pictures I need.

If you choose to accept this assignment, you can look forward to lump-sum retainer payments of £250,000 every three months, dependent on the success of the operations before that time. The photographs you take will be exclusively for me, owned by me and used by me. You will not be paid 'per shot'.

I look forward to your responses.
Jonathan

P.S. All for one, and one for all, as they say: if one of you is out, then the deal is off. Remember: no partnership = no deal.

* * *

I looked at Raymont as he read the letter. Then he began to chuckle.

'Jonathan's a trickster, isn't he? If he wasn't a bloody Aussie, I'd have him down as CIA.'

My hands were sweating. I was beginning to feel like Jonathan's little puppet. And now I was going to be forced to work with the most hated photographer in England, if not the world.

But maybe that was still better than slinking back to St. Albans with nothing; owing a fortune I'd never be able to pay off.

Of course it was better.

'OK, we need to talk about this.' I took hold of the situation and felt a surge of the go-getting Natalie de Silva streak returning. 'We need to talk about the reasons why you're here. I need to know your side of everything that's happened to you, before I can commit to this. Nobody is going to want to know me if I do this with you, right now or in the future, but I need it and so do you. So what I need more than anything is to hear what you've got to say to defend yourself against what you did.'

Raymont gave me a look that seemed to suggest that he was impressed, before turning back to old Guiseppe behind the counter.

'Guiseppe, my friend, could we pay for our coffee? We're retiring for something a little stronger. My beautiful companion here needs a little enlightening on the realities of life, friend.'

In a few moments, we were out of the door into the chilly, dirty swirl of the London dust, and, walking a few paces apart, huddled into clothes and our anonymity for a few minutes more.

19

'So why does Jonathan think you've been wronged in some way, like me, then? As far as I've ever heard, you were not the victim of your situation, you were the cause. You're gonna have to make this good, I'm telling you, or that card is going to be ripped into tiny pieces and flushed down the toilet.'

I'd decided that attack was the best form of defence whilst I'd walked behind Marcus Raymont down side streets that he appeared to know very well. It wasn't a pretty area, but it was clearly somewhere he'd been before. Knowing what I did about his past, that didn't surprise me. Despite myself, I was impressed at his knowledge of London, a place that I only knew from the back of a limo. I found myself a little scared, but also thrilled about the seediness of the areas we were walking through.

A 'heard it all before' look came over Raymont's features as he settled into the padded burgundy seating in a dark corner of The Queen's Head, somewhere down a back alley in Camden Town. He'd unwrapped his face completely now, obviously feeling safe in a pub that he'd clearly spent a lot of time in before, and he was actually quite a good looking guy, in a sort of chiselled, posh, English, Russell Crowe, older man kind of way.

Part of me was repulsed to be even sitting next to him, but part of me desperately wanted to hear his story. He had been a famous man for much of my teenage years, hated, reviled and despised by many, but also the subject of a great deal of intrigue from everybody who heard his story, especially me.

I'd been eleven years old when it happened, a budding young photographer, and the events of that night on TV were massively important to me, in a slightly different way from everybody else. It was the photography part that cut right to my heart. For others, there were other elements of the story that were more haunting.

I could still remember clearly the newsflash on TV one night in the middle of *EastEnders*, and the way that summer evening seemed to last forever. All the channels had abandoned their usual programming to cut to live coverage of the horrible events for the rest of the night. The de Silvas, like every other family in England, were glued to their sets long past midnight and well into the following weeks.

'Well it's all a long time ago now,' Raymont sighed, 'but I think you should know a little background to our "offer" here, before I tell you the rest, which I'm prepared to do. All I ask is that you give me a fair hearing and listen carefully before you judge. OK?'

I couldn't imagine that anything could possibly change

my mind about him, but I nodded curtly.

'OK, thanks. I appreciate that. So why am I here and why has Jonathan set us both up like this? Well first of all, what with the court case and the media interest, things have only just started to calm down for me now. I've been with Jonathan's agency for a long time, and he's the only guy who has stuck by me through all of this.'

Raymont lit a cigarette and exhaled away from me. I assumed it was for my benefit. At least he had some manners.

'I owe Jonathan for standing by me. I haven't had any work for several years now, but he has helped me financially to stay afloat. Without that help, I would've been bankrupt and out on the street. He's a good man, in some ways.'

He smiled as he said it. I could tell he wasn't convinced that he could trust Jonathan completely. I knew what he meant.

'But Jonathan owes me a great deal as well, which is something you might not be aware of. I presented him with much of his success in the early days, the eighties, when photography was still a noble art.' Raymont smirked and inhaled deeply. 'I believed I was going to be a great photographer, but then I started taking pictures of famous people, and Jonathan and I realised that my pictures were a goldmine. The public wanted dirt. They no longer expected to worship the people they'd made famous. They expected to see them humiliated, too.'

I clenched my hands tightly in front of me on the table.

It was like hearing my own story being read. Surely I couldn't share a history with a man like this?

'Jonathan got all my best pictures in his early days. We were partners. I got the scoop, he got the story printed, and we shared the money. He built his business on my images, and I built my reputation. Such as it now is. Not much of a reputation, is it?'

He let out a laugh that died as it left his mouth. I almost felt a touch of sympathy for him, but not for long.

'OK, then,' I said slowly. 'So you were a good pap in your time, because you made a lot of money. Big deal. What made you turn into the devil?' I was not going to let him manipulate this situation. I wanted answers.

'Ah, the devil in me. Hmm, an interesting label. And the devil in you, Natalie? Is the devil in you too? I've got nothing to hide, my dear, just ask anything, as long as you don't think there's only one devil in this world.'

He took a slug of his G and T, while I considered the cold facts, wondering where to start. I was glad I'd ordered mineral water. I wanted a clear head.

The news had crackled across the TV screen. First there was the explosion and sinking of the princess's speedboat after a violent crash with another boat, then the small pieces of white wreckage floating on the turquoise sea off Cannes. A whole flotilla of boats was at the scene, visible from the shore in fuzzy video images and local television station pictures. On screen we could see people hauling things out of the water, helicopters hovering above the carnage. It would be a miracle if any of the passengers were still alive.

The young princess had been on board with a group of other teenagers with connections to European royalty and beyond; a bunch of rich kids on a night out on the French Riviera, travelling by boat from their private villa to the clubs that lined the jetty. The princess was only sixteen years old, most of her friends a little older. At that stage, there was no news about who had survived, just an unofficial list of who had been on the boat.

Then there was the wait, as we wondered if anyone could have survived what we had seen, especially the young girl whose life we had watched enviously and with excitement as she grew from a chubby little girl into a beautiful young woman. She had been fortunate to be born into the royal family, but she was also wildly popular, both with the youngsters who saw a new type of royal emerging, somebody who was at least a bit more down to earth, and with the newspapers, who now had someone to fill their pages with on a daily basis. She was vivacious, outgoing, sweet-natured and royal. She sold copies.

We had all wanted to be her: to be sixteen and rich and pretty and have the pick of gorgeous posh boys, too. What we didn't know was how the attention could turn sour, how it could all go horribly wrong, and how the constant scrutiny she was under for our benefit was actually a bit like torture. She couldn't go anywhere or do anything without everyone finding out. It was a royal soap opera.

And then the news that we had been waiting for came

through. It was one of those 'where were you when X happened?' moments. I'd felt the wave of emotion too, as I watched the coverage on TV – even though I'd never met the girl. And I wasn't alone.

Later, we learned about the chasing paparazzi photographers who'd been following the princess for months, in their cars, on their motorbikes and now, finally, in their boats: how they'd weaved around, cut up and generally harassed the driver of the royals' boat and hunted the kids down so that they could get the best pictures, until it was all bound to end up with a loss of control and a crash.

And how those photographers had killed the princess.

For weeks afterwards, the press and their paparazzi photographers were hunted themselves. Photographers were nowhere to be seen, except for one man, who was on the news and on the front page of every newspaper; the same papers that days ago were using his pictures of other celebs.

Yes, Marcus Raymont, who, after reports from eye witnesses who had tracked the events offshore through binoculars and seen the chasing pack in the seconds before the crash, was accused of deliberately swerving across the front of the princess's boat, trying to force it to slow down or stop. It was at that moment that the other driver had apparently lost control.

Worse even than the princess's fatal accident, for me, as an eleven-year-old who loved photography and with her whole future ahead of her, was the news that came out within hours of the announcement of her death. That a leading member of the top flight paparazzi could have been responsible. He exploited the horrific events without lifting a finger to help. Surely nobody halfway human could do a thing like that?

But it was true. From the shore, people had seen it happen. It wasn't just Marcus, of course, there were other photographers in the water too. But it was his name that was called out – and flashed all over the front pages. Marcus Raymont was the ringleader.

I looked up from my drink.

'I don't know what to say to you. It's still almost too much to take in or talk about.'

'I can tell you one thing,' Marcus said, pushing his hand through his hair wearily. 'Had you been in my position, you would have done the same.'

I gave him a look of complete contempt. 'Get over yourself. I wouldn't, I never would.' I practically spat out the words. I felt that I was doing what a million people had wanted to do for many years to this man. It felt good, very good, to surrender to that wave of emotion again after all those years, although a nagging doubt crossed my mind as I spoke.

'Oh, save it, Goody Two-shoes,' Marcus said drily. 'Shut up and listen.' And all of a sudden he was animated – or perhaps you'd call it passionate. Either way, he certainly stopped me in my self-righteous little tracks.

'I know your history,' he said bluntly. 'I know why you're

sitting here and what started it, so I know, if you really dig deep into your soul, that you'll understand. And I did what any good photographer does when faced with a choice between the photograph and the situation. I chose the photograph. As did you. You can't deny it.'

I flushed red – it was getting to be a habit these days – and felt a prickle of something like shame inside me. Technically yes, I had done the same thing. But in my case, lives weren't at stake. Nobody died because of me. Before I could reply Marcus continued, his voice becoming lower, more monotonous, almost as if he was weary of saying the same thing that he had said countless times before.

'I was in Cannes for the week, following the princess's party all around the place. They'd been at the charity event that day, loving us taking their pictures, milking it. All the younger ones were there, and they wanted to be seen doing the good stuff, but we had inside information that they were heading for the clubs later, and they didn't want any then. Because the princess was underage, there would be certain narcotics going around, not to mention a few young playboy drug users. Why should they have it both ways? I wasn't going to miss out on a picture like that. It was in the public interest. So I got in our hired boat and I followed them. We all followed them. It was normal down there, it was just what you did and they knew that.'

He paused again. This time I didn't want to interrupt. Marcus drank further down his glass and then continued, more quietly still.

'We were a couple of minutes out of their private jetty, coming round the coast in front of the beach at Cannes. The boat they were in was speeding but ours was faster. Their driver was trying to outrun us, but he wasn't experienced. I've been doing it for years and I was the designated driver for the day, although I still had my cameras round my neck, ready to fire off a couple of shots at some point. It was a normal chase, but for some reason it all went wrong. Their driver just veered right into our space to cut us off. It was totally unnecessary and there was nothing we could do. I tried to outgun them to get out of the way, so I hit the throttle, and just as I did, the two boats collided. It was like a knife slicing through butter, because we were so much bigger than they were. The next thing I knew the boats had separated again and I looked back and there was fire everywhere and they were in the water. It was carnage. We were so lucky. They weren't.'

Raymont seemed to be almost in a trance. I believed what he was saying, because there had been video evidence at the trial that supported most of what he said, although the judge had also criticised the paparazzi for the way they had harassed the other boat.

'But the pictures at the scene? You really think that I would have taken those pictures? That was just disgusting. I couldn't have done that, whatever the picture was.'

It had been the question asked a million times, the subject of countless articles and television specials in the time since the princess's death, and always the conclusion was the same: Raymont and his partner were barbaric.

'Listen, Natalie. The only difference between you and me was that *maybe* I could have saved a life. But if you've ever seen the pictures I took that night, you would know why I didn't help.'

He appeared to falter for a moment. I prompted him again.

'Why?'

'I've photographed wars, assassinations, disasters, won awards for all that stuff, and I know when I see a dying person. I'm not a doctor, but I have some idea how much a body can withstand, and that night there was nobody in the water that was going to stay alive for more than a few minutes more, unless they were going to be hooked up to machines and become vegetables for the rest of their lives. I'm not saying I didn't want to help.' For a second, Marcus appeared to falter and looked down at the table, rubbing his eyes with his hand before continuing. 'I checked before I started shooting, in a split second. They were burned beyond help, drowning. I checked.'

Marcus was becoming emotional, I could feel, but trying not to show it in case he lost control. If this was an act, it was a very good one. His eyes narrowed as he continued.

'And then I was looking at all of that through my lens too. In close-up. You know the privilege that that gives us. You understand, I know, that we can see things clearer, much clearer, than anyone else can. Of course it was hard not to help drag the bodies out and all that, but I knew, and I still know, that there was no hope at all in that place. It was devastating, just like photographing anybody who is dying. I've taken a lot of pictures like that. It doesn't get any easier.'

I was silent, digesting all that I'd been told. I knew I might have to reassess my opinion of this man. I did remember the feeling he had described, just a few months earlier, in the milliseconds before the shutter was released for the first shot, before my pictures became living things. It is the moral dilemma for every photographer: is it better that this photograph exists or not? I didn't even want to think about the pictures he had taken and what he had seen.

I still had questions though. I still needed more evidence that there was another side to what I'd seen and heard about that night.

'OK, but what about you selling the pictures? They were on the Internet within two hours of the crash, weren't they? How can you justify that?'

Raymont rolled his eyes. 'Natalie. Get in the real world, will you? You're sitting in this pub with me today because you sold an "immoral" picture and everything that's happened to you since came directly from it. What difference is there, in reality, between you and me? Somebody paid you, you sold your soul. You ruined lives. Somebody paid me. I sold my soul. I ruined lives. And we both made a hell of a lot of money. Maybe now I would do things differently, maybe not; maybe you would change what you did too. But all those years ago I was working for my reputation. I wanted the money that I was going to get from what I thought was the most important photograph of the decade, maybe even ever. I didn't stop to think.'

I had no answer for that. He was right. We were the same.

'And the way I've been treated by the media, and the courts and people in general, it's as if I'm some kind of devil, you're right. We've got that in common. But what have we done wrong, except for being used by the people who paid us to do what they wanted and go as far as they demanded, so that they got everything and we lost it all? Think about it. We're victims – just as much as the people we're supposed to have hurt.'

There *were* a lot of connections between us, some I didn't like to think about because they made me too ashamed. Raymont had taken things a step further than I had all those months ago, maybe further than I ever would, but who was to say that I wouldn't have done exactly the same thing if I had been in his situation? That thought scared me a little.

I took out my mobile, flipped it open so that Raymont knew exactly what I was doing, and called Jonathan.

20

'*Marcus Raymont?* For God's sake, girl, do you not know what that man has done?'

Although standing in my mum's pinny and finishing the washing up didn't exactly lend my dad much authority, it was the closest he'd been to losing it in years. I was scared he might start to throw things.

'This is just the final straw, Natalie. You've gone too far.'

He slammed a wet wooden spoon down on to the work surface and bubbles flew off into the air.

'Dad, this is my big chance to sort out my debts to Jonathan,' I told him, batting a stray bubble out of my face. 'I've met Marcus, and there's so much about everything that happened that you don't know. Besides, I don't have much choice. I'm going to take the job.'

I had decided to tell my parents straight away. It had taken me the hour or so journey back on the train from King's Cross to put together a plan for breaking the news. That had fallen apart in the first few seconds. I hadn't expected my dad to be quite as angry as he was. Maybe

I'd underestimated what the last few months had taken out of them.

Then Mum spoke up. 'Darling, please don't do this. You know that we can find other ways to pay off your debts. Grandma has some savings she can give us to help towards it. She told me . . .'

I could see that Mum was about to start crying. I would no doubt get the blame for that as well.

This wasn't going well at all.

I stood with my back to the door that led from the kitchen into the garden, feeling that at least I might have a getaway option if things took even more of a turn for the worse. I was hemmed in everywhere else, Mum at the door into the hall and Dad at the sink.

'Kathleen, please don't get upset. I will sort this out.' Dad turned to me again. 'See what you've done to your mother? This is all your fault, Natalie. If you had listened to us in the first place about those awful pictures you took, none of this would have happened. You would be going to university in September and we wouldn't be facing financial ruin and utter humiliation because of the company you choose to keep.'

There was a vein popping out on Dad's forehead just above his right eye as he spoke. He had a point, of course, but I couldn't see any other way out of my mess. He had to see that. There was no way I was letting my parents take on all that debt. I was a big girl now and I wanted to sort it out myself. They'd just have to accept it.

'You've already caused enough trouble for this family with what you were getting up to in London,' Dad raged on. 'We tried to let you get on with it and not interfere, let you make your own mistakes, but you've let us down so much, Natalie. We can't have this any more.'

I stared at him, trying to give the impression that I was calm. On the inside I was churning.

Dad seemed to calm down a little. He leaned against the sink, and said, seriously, 'It's got to stop, Natalie. We had already decided that one more thing would be the last, and now you've presented us with no alternative.'

'What do you mean?' I said, confused.

My mum cast an anxious look at Dad across the room.

'John, darling, please don't say anything too drastic. We can sort this out if we just sit down and talk about it. Like we always have done. Maybe there's a way out of it this time?'

There were now tears running down my mum's face. She usually only got like this during soppy movies. My mum and dad never argued – except over me, of course. And this was just another Natalie de Silva situation.

It hurt to see her like that, but there was no going back now.

'Mum, there's no point in us talking about it any more than we have because I'm going to take the offer and I'm going to go back to London, clear my debts and start again. Don't take this the wrong way, but I don't want to live in St Albans all my life – I want just a bit more . . . you know?'

Mum's mouth hung open and Dad turned away to the sink again. I could see his reflection in the kitchen window, but he seemed to be refusing to turn around and even look at me now. His head was turned to the side and he looked like a defeated, deflated man.

'Very well, Natalie.' He spoke slowly. 'If this is what you want, then this is what you'll have to do. But we cannot support you in it, and neither will any other member of this family. As far as we're concerned, you're not a part of this family any more. We do not want to be associated with people like Raymont, or anybody else like him.'

'John . . .' my mum broke in. 'Please, John, we have to at least try . . .' Mum's voice trailed off. I shook my head at both of them, imploring Mum to understand what I had to do.

'No Kathleen, it's gone too far.' My dad turned and looked at Mum. 'If Natalie thinks that what we've tried to give her all her life is beneath her, then it's better that she goes. Maybe some day she will change and realise that family is what is important, not all this running around and trying to be famous or whatever it's all about.'

Mum said nothing, but she wouldn't meet my eyes. She just stared down at the lino, then finally murmured, 'It's better for all of us if you go, Natalie.'

I stared at them. They would never understand.

'OK,' I said slowly. 'You mean that you want me to move out for a while, Dad? I was going to live in London anyway. Jonathan has got me a place.'

'No, that's not what we mean.' Dad couldn't look me in the eye. 'We want you to leave and not come back until you've changed. Until you know the right thing to do. You're making this very difficult for your mum and me. But there's no other way. You're not welcome back here, not the way you are at the moment.'

I was stunned.

'Now please go. Quickly. Pack and go. Don't make it any harder than it already is.'

'Mum? Do you want this too?' I'd always been able to divide my parents and rule the house. It was usually the last resort, but it always worked.

Dad looked up at Mum and held out his arms. She walked quickly across the kitchen and folded into him, crying.

There was no sound in the kitchen except the humming of the fridge-freezer in the corner. It used to drive me mad. Today, even though it seemed to be more like a jumbo jet coming in to land in the silence of the room, I only cared about the sound my mum had to make, to keep our family together.

'Your dad's right, Natalie. You need to go. We've just had enough of all this. We can't take it. We want you to change, but if you won't, then we can't support you any more.'

So, my mild-mannered parents were finally taking a stand. Trying to teach me a lesson I'd never forget, no doubt. I could see their reasoning, I suppose, but I'd made my decision; I'd just have to live with the consequences.

Silently, I walked through the hallway and up the stairs to my room. I packed a few items of clothing into a couple of suitcases and left the rest behind. I wouldn't need anything more where I was going. The time had come to get myself back on track, back to where I had been, the top. If it took everything I had, I would do it, because nothing else mattered to me any more. I told myself my parents would come round in the end, they always did. They would just have to put up with the way things were until then. It was their loss.

Half an hour later I was in a taxi heading back to London.

21

For the next three months, I was on probation. Jonathan told me he wanted me to learn the business of being a true pap. If I showed that I had the 'balls', as he put it, I would be in as an equal with Marcus.

What I needed to do was to prove that I could do whatever it took to get the picture, the killer photograph that changed somebody's life, and made a lot of money for Jonathan.

I knew I could do it, because I'd done it before, but I didn't realise that there was so much to learn. When I'd got my pictures the previous September, I was plain lucky. I'd stumbled across the story. Now I had to learn the skills needed to source the story, the patience to wait for the perfect moment, the techniques required to position myself where other paps would love to be. Luckily I had the best teacher possible; or the worst, depending on how you looked at it.

My first assignment was to dramatically change my image. I nearly cried when the hairdresser cut off my long brown mane, but it had to be done and I could see that the disguise was perfect. I was a short-haired tomboy, with a whole wardrobe of street gear ordered for me by a trustworthy member of JD's agency. Now I had street trainers instead of my designer shoes and wore high street jeans again. Even if the press had been remotely interested now, they would have found it hard to recognise the new Natalie.

Two days later I was sent on my first job with Marcus.

He picked me up at 5 a.m. in a sporty looking car that looked expensive but not too showy. I guessed it was for speed without being too obvious and I was right. Marcus told me the first rule of the extreme paparazzi, the group we were going to join: anonymity at all costs, until the moment of truth. I'd spent the previous day working with Marcus in a small park down the road from the flat Jonathan had got for me in Bayswater, loving every minute of holding, testing and shooting my new cameras. Once we'd safely stored them in the back of the car, Marcus told me to get some more sleep and I dropped off. I wasn't used to such early starts.

By the time I woke up we were in the car park of some service station on the M40. Marcus shook my arm to get me to focus.

'OK, wake up properly and listen carefully. You have a lot to take in, and quickly.'

Marcus fiddled with some wires on the centre shelf between us, lifting a box to reveal two brand new, top spec mobiles.

'GPS technology, instant messaging for silent but immediate conversation, camera and video, the latest top-speed net access and technology for information gathering on the go. Everything you need in your mobile and more. I wish we'd had all this twenty-five years ago. One each. Don't lose it.'

I gave him a withering look.

'I won't. What's all this?'

I pointed at the tightly bound roll of papers he had stuffed into the plastic wells in between us.

'Lists of number plates used by celebs, take-off and landing times for private planes and helicopters today at the airfields around London, schedules from PAs of agents; you name it, we've got it. Oh, and the plans for the buildings and grounds of a nearby country mansion.'

I flicked idly through a couple of the pages.

'We're not turning into burglars too, are we?'

'Nah, don't worry, no breaking and entering.' Marcus laughed.

'Right, so what are we actually doing in this horrible little service station? We're obviously not getting a KFC bucket.'

'All will become clear, Natalie. Don't worry, we've got a target, we're just waiting for the signal. Patience, my dear. It's the necessary virtue of every pap. Sometimes you will have to wait a whole day, maybe two, before you can get the shot you are looking for.'

I settled back down into my seat to wait.

'I'm not very good at waiting. I'll have to work on it,' I said jokingly.

But within a couple of minutes, Marcus's mobile vibrated and started to flash. 'No audible alerts please,' he reminded me, before taking the call.

'Sure, OK, got it. No problem. We'll be there in five minutes. Beautiful.' He flicked off the phone and turned to me with a wide smile.

'What's happening then?' In spite of myself I could feel a swelling sense of excitement. I could sense that Marcus was buzzing, too.

'We're on. I'll tell you as we drive. You need to listen carefully.'

Within minutes I had been given the breakdown of our task – or 'test' – given as a challenge by Jonathan to prove ourselves worthy of his employment. Jenna Johnson, former member of girl group Stunned and popular winner of the celebrity reality TV show *Lost in the Desert*, was a client of Jonathan's. I'd met her a few times when I was on the way up. Apparently Jonathan looked upon her almost as a daughter, the child he'd never had. He was very protective of her and her emotional well-being.

Jenna's husband, Steven McAllum, had recently quit the UK's top pop band and gone solo and they had two small children from their short marriage. Three days earlier, Jenna had called Jonathan, almost hysterical, asking for his help. She had seen a tabloid news story about McAllum, and needed to know if it was true that he was having an affair with an actress he had worked with on a recent number one hit duet. It was sad. I had met Steven, and I knew that there was every chance he was playing away. He had attempted to get me into bed just before Christmas.

'So what's the plan?' I was happy to take part in this one.

If it was true, the guy deserved what was coming to him. If it wasn't, it wouldn't bother me anyway. Both Steven and Jenna had been the worst publicity-seeking couple since Brett and Kassie Ballentine. Maybe Jonathan knew that this would be an easy way in for me?

'I'll park up down here and we'll take it from there.'

Marcus pulled into a lay-by, which was framed on all sides by high hedges, enclosing this country road from the weak spring sunshine. We had passed through a couple of small and pretty South Oxfordshire villages, full of lovely old cottages at the centre and big newer mansions on the fringes. We were right on the edge of another.

'Old Edgerton. Home of the famous celebrity agent Neil Harmon, whose house is apparently being used by a young couple with a lot to hide, who just happen to be on his books. And just around the corner from here as well. How convenient.'

He slid the garden and building plan out of the pack of papers I'd seen before. The whole house and garden was on one large folded sheet.

'Now, I want you to skirt around the back of the house and meet me, here.' He pointed at the plan. 'There's an alarm system, but it doesn't stretch further than these boundaries. If all goes to plan, we won't need to go inside them anyway. I'm going to go the other way round, check for security and make sure any far-away neighbours can't see what we're up to. Keep your head down and keep in contact until we meet at the back. From what I'm told, this place has great angles from the rear.' He paused. 'A bit like you, my dear.'

I was almost concentrating too hard to understand the comment. Then it hit me, so I hit *him*, firmly on the arm.

'You can't help yourself can you, old man. Your heart might give out if you start with all that stuff.'

'Ah I could teach you a thing or two, Natalie, don't you worry. But let's leave all that for later. For now, we need to concentrate on getting the shots. Do you understand the plan?'

'Of course I do. And no. It's you that needs to concentrate. I've been doing that anyway.'

Two minutes later I was padding through an open field to the left of the boundary of the agent's house. Luckily it was a dry, warm day, and it didn't take long to get my bearings.

The house was surrounded on three sides by greenery, a beautiful spot. The front of the house was only a few metres from the road, which left me wondering how anyone could see this as a good hideout. I guess the guy had never thought an entertainment agent would need to hide.

Unfortunately for Neil Harmon, and his clients inside, the road wasn't their only problem. A relatively thin line of tall bushes and trees was all that protected the boundary at the side and back, and as I walked steadily along, dipping my head to keep out of range of the upper windows of the house, every few metres I would catch a brief glimpse of garden through gaps in the vegetation. This was going to be easy.

I'd kept my phone line connected to Marcus's as instructed and heard his quiet voice through my Bluetooth headset.

'I'm in place round the back. Nothing going on on this side. What about you?'

'No, all clear here too. Meet you in one minute.'

Literally as soon as I'd finished speaking I hit the corner spot where Marcus was already hiding, squatting against the dirt track with his camera bag open, fixing his lenses and checking the light.

I ducked down with him and did the same.

'I love this moment. Always the perfect time. It's the anticipation. It's like sex,' he said, chuckling, 'only with sex, the reality matches the anticipation. With me anyway, of course.'

I glanced across at him, amazed he had thought he could get away with such a lame comment.

'God, Marcus, you're embarrassing. Those kinds of lines went out in 1967, you know. Can we just get on with it?'

I wasn't going to fall out with him, but he needed to be reminded of why we were here. Regularly. This wasn't a game. It was my future I was working for.

In a few seconds we had set up the tripods, the lenses and zooms. Now it was time to wait.

'They're in the top right-hand bedroom, the one with the balcony. Our information is that they've been having breakfast every morning out there on the terrace, taking advantage of our early spring warm spell.'

'How the hell did you get that kind of information?' I asked, incredulously.

'I have friends everywhere, Nat. That's the job. You infiltrate. You ask the right people the right questions. You will learn about all this stuff. Anyway, the farmer across the field didn't know who the people in the big house were. All he knew was that a grand was a lot of money to confirm that people were sitting out there each day when he was driving his tractor around.'

I sniggered.

'And to call a mobile number when the curtains opened today. A thousand quid's a lot of cows in his world.'

'Jesus Christ. I'm glad you weren't around when I was a celebrity.'

'Who said I wasn't?' Marcus looked at me for a few seconds, before grinning and turning back to his camera.

It took another forty minutes for Steven and his actress girlfriend to walk out on to the terrace, embrace, another forty seconds for his marriage to be over with a loving kiss, in full view of our cameras. As the shutters clicked and the images began to store in my digital camera's memory card, I thought about how he would feel when he woke up tomorrow and read the papers. The end of his marriage and possibly his career. In the space of a few seconds.

I focused again as his hands moved further around the woman's waist, grasping her firmly and reaching up for her breast.

'Gotcha,' I mouthed silently to myself and clicked again.

22

I enjoyed myself during those few weeks in London. I lived a quiet life, and managed to stay anonymous, going out for milk and chocolate when I needed it at the local Spar and generally keeping out of harm's way the best I could.

I even managed to fit in some 'proper' photography around the pap shoots that happened very irregularly, sometimes once a week, sometimes three or four. Some days I would go off into Hyde Park, or down to the Thames, and shoot anything that I saw that made me shiver or woke up my brain for a few moments. As spring turned into summer, London stopped being a nightmare and became somewhere I could be myself and relax properly.

Whatever happened, I kept my new mobile close to me, and lived inside my head for a while, with no distractions. Several times I tried to call my parents, but they wouldn't listen to anything I tried to say. They just asked me not to call again.

Ravi sent a couple of emails, talking about how nervous he was about his exams coming up, how Evie was panicking too in that special Evie kind of way that involved all-night phone sessions and eating loads of bacon sandwiches at two in the morning.

It was good to hear from him, and we both avoided the subject of the day we'd gone to our old pub and ended up leaving in a hurry. It was too much for us to start up with it all over again, and my emails back never revealed exactly what I was doing in London. I just told him that Jonathan had provided me with a couple of opportunities that I couldn't refuse, if I was to try and rebuild my career and get back to the place I'd been before. We never spoke on the phone. It was almost as if there was an unwritten rule that we should keep things simple, keep our friendship alive, at least, and wait for the next opportunity for us to make things right, if we ever could.

I was at Camden Market one day when Marcus called with some news.

'Nat, we've got something to do tonight. You have to get yourself ready as usual, except there are some extra preparations you need to do.'

I was used to bantering with Marcus by now, and I thought maybe he was winding me up again.

'Marcus, I always prepare for our dates together, you know that. I'll make sure I put on that special Superdrug £2.99 perfume that I know you love. Will that be OK?'

'I'm serious, Nat. Jonathan says this is the final test.'

It was not like Marcus to miss a chance at some harmless flirting. I realised this must be the real deal.

'Everything up until now has been Jonathan's way of making sure we could still hack the basics. But he's preparing something else for us, something big, if we can get through tonight. If we get this one right tonight, then we're on the proper main job. He says it could be the biggest story for years.'

Marcus was breathless with excitement. I could almost imagine what he must have been like on the night of the big crash, starting up the boat, swerving out towards the princess's yacht, rushing to make the picture. It was one big adventure for him, and I'd started to get hooked now myself. I moved away to a corner, behind a stall selling T-shirts of Kurt Cobain and tacky beaded jewellery, so that I could talk more privately.

'Right, what's this big test all about then? Do you have the details?'

'Not yet. We'll find out everything when we're on the way. All I know is that I have to wear clothes suitable for a night out in the West End, and you're to get your hair cut as short as possible before this evening, and wear comfortable, flat black shoes. You're going to be on your feet all night, I'm told. OK?'

Great, I thought. He gets to be party boy and I get to be . . . a boy.

'I'll pick you up dead on five,' he said. 'We've got some driving to do, not much, but I have to take you somewhere on the way. That's all I know, we'll find out more later.'

'OK, I'll see you at five. Bye.'

I pressed 'End' and glanced around me, feeling as if I was in some kind of spy movie. I knew nobody could have heard Marcus's words, but they still felt embarrassing to me in some way, a little dirty, despite the excitement. In a matter of seconds though, my head was clear. I strode out of the passageway between the stalls and on to the main pathway, into the busy crowded market, anonymous again, but feeling like the whole world could see my secret.

23

We were halfway to Chelsea when Marcus's mobile started to vibrate in the tray between our seats. He picked up using his hands-free and then switched to speaker so that I could hear too.

'Good evening, you two. Hope you're enjoying this lovely warm evening. I've got something just a little bit special for you tonight.'

I felt a bit like one of Charlie's Angels with Jonathan as Bosley, issuing our next assignment.

Jonathan paused for effect. He was such a drama queen sometimes.

'Just spit it out will you, old man. I'm stuck in a jam in the middle of Kensington High Street and I can do without the amateur dramatics,' Marcus said, turning to me and rolling his eyes. It felt like we were real partners, at last, just us against the world. It's funny how things can change.

'All right, keep your hair on, Marcus, whatever you've still got left.' There was some particularly Australian laughter at the other end until it came to rest and he seemed ready to talk.

'I'll give you all the details in a minute. But first of all, you both need to consider very seriously whether you are prepared to do this at all. What you're about to do could have big implications for the whole country, not just sell a lot of newspapers and make me a lot of money. Although that's always something to consider.'

'Go on,' I said, 'we can take it. I'm sure we'll cope.' I was impatient to hear what we had to do. I'd heard enough and done enough in the last few weeks to feel I could do anything to anybody famous without feeling too much regret.

'Right, then here goes. Tonight, my terrible twosome, you are going to the twenty-first birthday party of the second in line to the British throne. There you will attempt to take the first pictures ever seen of the prince himself, kissing, or fondling, or whatever princes do these days, his beautiful, slim, attractive and incredibly rich girlfriend. This is the girl, who, if my information is correct, and I have no doubt that it is, will be the next queen of England, the love of that young man's life.'

I looked at Marcus, who was gripping the wheel tightly.

'If you succeed in getting what we're after, the royal family will have a public relations disaster on their hands. There've been no reports about this girl anywhere, simply because the prince and one or two of his closest advisors have used every trick in the book to avoid us finding out. Even the rest of the royals have no idea. They met abroad, and they've managed to keep it all totally out of sight until now.'

I broke in.

'Jonathan, so what if the prince has a girlfriend? It's not like he's not allowed to. He's had loads. What's the big deal?'

'Well, there are quite a few big deals, Natalie. She's secret because she's completely inappropriate. Not only because she's fails on the "posh bird with funny teeth from Gloucestershire who went to the same public school as the good old prince" test, but also because she's the daughter of a Russian oil baron with alleged mafia connections, who is currently facing thirty years in prison for his part in billion-dollar money laundering schemes across the past fifteen years. And there's more.'

I whistled slowly. 'This all sounds like the plot of a Bond movie. I can see what all the fuss is about, I guess. What else is there?'

I looked across again at Marcus. The traffic was moving now and fairly quickly. For some reason, though, he wasn't responding as part of the conversation at all. In fact, he looked very pale, like he was about to throw up. Jonathan started speaking again, so I tried to concentrate above the noise of the car's engine.

'Well plenty. Secondly, she's a Catholic. Catholics are still not allowed to be monarchs in this country or be married to them. That could give a few old duffers some heart attacks and provoke a constitutional crisis if we handle it properly. And third, probably best of all, this girl has not been a good girl all her life. In fact, she's been very bad. I have in front of me some very, very incriminating pictures of her from her days at private school. Think hard drugs and lots of sex and you have the picture.'

I had to hand it to Jonathan. He was certainly on top of his information-gathering procedures.

'And nobody has even suspected they're together?'

'Nobody. There'll be hell to pay when the Family finds out.'

I shook my head, quickly digesting all this information and glanced again at Marcus. He was staring straight ahead as the car picked up speed, when I suddenly realised the car in front was coming closer and the traffic had stopped dead again. Only we were not stopping at all.

'Marcus!' I shouted and grabbed the wheel, twisting it to try to avoid a collision. Suddenly Marcus seemed to wake up and the car juddered to a halt.

'What the hell are you doing? We nearly ran into them, man,' I shrieked. 'Get a grip! Pull over.'

Marcus hauled the car out of the traffic and into a tiny side street where we were able to park for a moment on double yellow lines.

'Jesus! Marcus, are you all right?' I rubbed my shoulders where the seatbelt straps had bitten into me.

Marcus stared at the dashboard.

'You don't get it, do you?' he said so quietly that I almost couldn't hear him.

'Get what, you freak? That you nearly killed us?'

'The job, Natalie. The prince? Destroying his life, his

149

relationship? Creating a massive public problem for the whole country?'

'Yeah, so what? It's only another version of what we've been doing for weeks, just a bit bigger.'

I couldn't see the problem. What had happened to the man with no morals?

And then just as he spoke it hit me.

'A royal version of what we've been doing. The same royal family whose lives I was accused of messing up seven years ago.'

'Oh my God, and the prince,' I said, 'He's the . . .'

I started to speak, but the words died on me.

There was a moment's silence as I wondered how, or even whether, I should say the words.

Then from the mobile speaker I heard Jonathan's jolly, almost triumphant voice.

'Got it in one, Natalie: the dead princess's only brother.'

24

The pictures appeared two days later in the Sunday tabloids. Apparently there had been a legal argument that lasted a full twenty-four hours before they felt they could even use them, and obviously I could understand why.

By the time we got to the venue for the party, Marcus was himself again. It was just a temporary attack of guilt, he told me, never to be repeated.

I was dressed in a frumpy waitress's outfit and Marcus was in his penguin suit. We must have looked a sight when we got out of the car. As we parted, I took Marcus's hand.

'We can still pull out of this if you want to. I'll do whatever you want to do.'

He looked down for a second at the pavement before raising his eyes from under his bushy old-man eyebrows. I saw a twinkle in them. I knew it would be fine.

We co-ordinated our attacks so that we were able to keep in full contact from backstage and front-of-house. Despite the attentions of everybody from his friends to his minders, we knew that the prince would be retiring to a back room that had been prearranged by one particular minder and the catering company boss. There was a requirement for a waitress to guard the room. It was a good thing that the prince had minders who were always on the look-out for extra cash to add to their personal agendas against what they felt was a certain class of woman.

The pictures were easy. Marcus slipped into the room in advance and fixed a motion sensor panoramic camera in the perfect corner position. All I had to do was photograph the two young lovers from behind using a micro cam on my lapel as they entered the room, so proving that they had not been set up and that they had indeed chosen to go in together.

Once the meeting was over, I rushed to check the camera. The pictures were fantastic. They were not crystal clear, but we had got what we needed. Nobody could say the prince was shy either. There were some pictures we kept back, partly as insurance, in case we ever needed to use them in future, and partly to spare the poor girl's blushes. I was quite envious. Along with a lot of girls my age, I'd always fancied the prince a bit at school, and there he was with her all over him like a rash. I guess they were at least happy the last time they saw each other.

We all met at Jonathan's house in Surrey the following morning. We entered the study, where he was sitting in a bright red leather chair, smoking a fat cigar, like he was king of the world.

'Well, you've both passed all the tests I've thrown at you. I couldn't ask for more. So I've decided to free you from your contracts and pay up immediately.'

Marcus and I looked at each other. Was he serious? This was supposed to be just the beginning, not the end.

'Jonathan, you said all this would lead to a bigger, better job. How can you just tell us it's all over?' I spat out the words with real venom. Jonathan Davies had turned me over before. I couldn't believe he was doing it again.

'Calm down, Natalie. I can't believe you've been holding your nerve through any of this work recently, with a volatile reaction like that.' He cleared his throat and stood up. Jonathan seemed to think he'd discovered a way to win the lottery over and over again by cheating the system, with no chance of ever being found out. Thinking about it, maybe he had.

'What do you expect me to say? I've done all this on the promise of more work, more money. You told us to expect more if we delivered and we have. Just so you can make a fortune at our expense? I can't believe you, Jonathan.'

Marcus caught my eye and grinned.

'What? What the hell are *you* laughing at?' I barked at him. 'You think this is funny or something? He's screwing you as well, you know.'

'This is what I have to put up with every time, Jonathan. I hope you understand now.' Marcus smiled at Jonathan knowingly. It made my blood boil, but he turned to me before I could speak.

'Just take a moment to think, would you? Jonathan never said anything about firing us. He just said the contract is cancelled and paid up. That means we're free to start a new, better contract. Don't you see?'

'But, he said . . .' I stopped, realising that I'd completely missed the point, and blushed a little. 'You mean you already knew?'

I was puzzled.

'Yes, I knew. Jonathan and I have already talked at length about what would happen next, if you turned out to be as good as he predicted. And you can breathe again. You are. But that's the last time I'll ever tell you.'

I didn't know whether to be furious with Marcus for going behind my back, or delighted with his words. I was still confused about the contracts though.

Jonathan stepped in.

'You're now free to work as freelancers. I will buy anything you produce, at market rates. No more retainers, no more fixed fees. From now on, you get paid the going rate and what you deserve. And one day soon, Natalie, I'll start to test the waters with the editors, see about getting you back on the other side of the lens. How does that sound?'

Jonathan finished with a flourish, his arms wide, a whisky glass clenched in one hand. I turned to Marcus, letting it all sink in. This was good news. I realised I could finally start earning properly and get back some of what I used to have. It would only be a matter of time before I could relaunch myself, with Jonathan's help.

'OK,' I said calmly. 'So what's next?'

Marcus gestured in the direction of the large desk at the end of the study wall.

'Maybe we should take a look, eh?'

We walked over to where a huge map had been unfolded, to cover half the desk. To the side were two ticket pouches with 'British Airways' written on them, a bulging packet of foreign currency, two brand new American Express credit cards and two pairs of Fendi sunglasses in their cases.

I looked at the name at the top of the map and grabbed for the airline tickets. Underneath my name, the destination was confirmed: Anguilla, in the British West Indies, better known as 'The Superstar Paradise Hideaway' and featured in every gossip column, in every magazine and newspaper in the world.

We were on our way to the Caribbean!

25

I sat on the balcony feeling the hot sun warming my face. It was all starting to flow back into me like some sort of fantastic intravenous drug: the first-class travel and accommodation, luxury fluffy towels, room service, chauffeur-driven cars. Perfect. Back to normal.

From inside my suite I heard the maid making the bed. I could get used to this again. This was what I'd worked so hard for. It was what I would get back, I was sure.

The phone on the table buzzed.

'Nat, would you like some croissants?'

It was Marcus. Every day of the trip so far he'd brought me breakfast. What a star he'd turned out to be. And if this was work, I wanted more.

'Sure – chocolate croissants if you can get them.'

I squinted as I took off my sunglasses, only to feel a hand resting lightly on my bare shoulder and Marcus's smiling face coming slowly into focus, one hand holding the bag of croissants.

'How's that for service?' He grinned and sat down on the chair next to my recliner, dropping the bag gently on my tummy.

It had been three days since we arrived, four since we had been given the news of this assignment. As usual, Jonathan had been keeping the details to himself. I didn't mind. Three days of holiday, relaxing and taking in the Caribbean sun without the stress of knowing what was coming, was fine by me.

'Heard anything from Jonathan?' I asked lazily, stretching, hoping not. I sat up and adjusted my bikini top. Marcus, pretending to be the perfect gentleman, studiously looked away into the distance and the waves lapping on the beach. I knew he was peeking really though.

'I'm afraid so. The holiday's over for the time being. Pity, isn't it?'

His teeth were so white when he smiled that you couldn't help staring at them. If I'd been ten years older . . . or maybe twenty. Then again, maybe not. I smiled to myself.

'Well it's been lovely, hasn't it? We knew it wasn't going to last for ever, but I'm actually ready to get to work, if you are. There's only so much sunbathing, swimming, eating, drinking and dancing a girl can do you know.' I sighed. 'Well, actually, let's forget the job and keep partying.'

I pulled a mock pouty face. Marcus smiled.

'If only we could. I could enjoy this view for ever.'

I wasn't sure which view he was talking about, but I was so used to his cheesy lines now that I knew the best way to deal with them was to ignore them.

'Come on then, what's the story? I've been wondering about it. A bit.'

'OK, come and sit at the table, I'll show you what we've got.'

With a stomach full of chocolate croissants and some hot coffee, I was ready for anything. We sat together and looked at the documents that had arrived by courier that morning from London.

Marcus fished out a colour photograph that was instantly recognisable.

'Shaqueel Brown, the most popular R 'n' B artist in the world in terms of record sales, downloads and earnings. Oh, and obviously the most world's most desirable man, according to the legendary amount of women he's slept with, divided by days in the year. You like?'

Marcus winked at me.

'Not really my kind of music, to be honest, but he's a good looking guy. I know a lot of girls who wouldn't say no. What about you?'

'Well, it's funny you should say that. No, not he's not really my cup of tea. And I prefer Old School Punk. My era, you know.'

I laughed. I could just see Marcus with his hair all glued up and spiky, bouncing up and down in some seedy little club with his brogues on.

'What's his nickname again? From that song he did. Oh yeah, he's "The Number One Stud" guy, isn't he?' I laughed. I threw some shapes with my hands. 'Check it out!'

Marcus smiled and shook his head.

'You young people today. I hardly have any idea what you're talking about most of the time.'

I punched his arm and got back to the point.

'So what about him? What's he done?'

I picked up a couple of the photographs on the table. There didn't seem to be much this guy didn't have. He was beautiful, his skin was flawless (obviously very well looked after with expensive products), his jaw line set square, his shoulders broad and in proportion. I could understand why a lot of girls went for him. As for his music, it was everywhere and had been for a couple of years now, topping both the US and UK single and album charts, time after time. This guy was a big star. Whatever the job was going to include, this was our biggest target yet.

'Well he hasn't really done anything, if you talk to the wrong people. Or the right people, if you're him.'

Marcus nodded at some photos of large homes practically hanging from the side of mountains. The pictures had clearly been taken using surveillance techniques, not open camerawork.

'He spends most of his time on Anguilla, because it's watertight for the stars. It's a British island, as you know, so the Americans feel very civilised here. It's also the place where they feel the safest, in their clifftop villas and secluded mansions. And the island protects the top celebrities that come here. They want them to come back. Why wouldn't they? They're making a lot of money from them.'

I picked up a photograph, taken openly in the street,

of Brown and his bodyguards scurrying across to a waiting car.

'He's got some serious protection, this guy, eh?'

'Yes, never without the two bozos in the sunglasses here, and here.' He pointed out the minders, as though it was hard to work out which ones they were.

'So come on, what's he done? Is it drugs? Secret lovers? HIV?' I was wracking my brains to come up with the angle that Jonathan had obviously uncovered from somewhere. There must be something big about this guy. For us to go after him, we needed something so damaging that it would be huge enough to give us a payday beyond anything the prince or any other past assignments had produced.

I looked up from the table at Marcus.

'All those girls he's slept with? The Number one Stud?' He paused.

'Yeah? What is it?' I pressed on.

Marcus paused again and smiled.

'All lies. He likes boys, not girls. Straight up.'

My mouth dropped open.

'Oh my God.'

'Or maybe "straight up" is the wrong expression to use in these circumstances?'

You could have caught a whole colony of mosquitoes in there by the time Marcus plopped my mouth shut with his finger.

'And it's up to us to prove it, my dear.'

26

Marcus had hired a 4×4 that morning, and we set out to uncover what we could about Shaqueel Brown, and find his whereabouts on the island.

Anguilla isn't a big place, but it's exclusive. As we drove from our hotel along the coast road, all I could see were perfect stereotypical views of a Caribbean island: white, unspoilt beaches dipping into a clear turquoise sea, shacks selling chicken and peas and mangos, bars and restaurants in makeshift buildings with everybody eating outside, coconuts everywhere. It was a little bit of heaven, and I could understand why the celebs would come here.

'Over there, on that hill, that's Exclusivity.' Marcus pointed. 'It's a rental villa for celebs. It's behind the trees so you can't really see it, let alone get to it, but trust me, it's there.' Marcus pulled over to the side of the road as we stared at the tree-lined hillside. 'They have fourteen staff who never speak to the press. It's in their contracts. Brad and Jennifer stayed there when they were together. seventy-five thousand dollars a week.'

I put my lips together as if to whistle and then felt a bit

stupid. I vowed to get myself a new version of 'impressed' for the future.

Marcus gunned the car again. A few moments later we came across a small group of shacks on the side of the road.

'OK, in a moment we'll be coming into The Valley. That's the island's capital, although it's hardly bigger than a small town back home. There's a police station, a small hospital and a few shops. Nothing else. Most of the life is out at the beach, although it's not like other Caribbean islands. There are no clubs, just bars, very exclusive hotels and top-class restaurants. We won't be eating in any though.' He glanced across at me to see my reaction. 'Four hundred dollars a head, most of them. I don't think Jonathan's expenses will stretch to that.'

I looked around in wonder from my high vantage point in the convertible 4×4. It was certainly a pretty place. But no clubs? It sounded like there wasn't much for a celebrity to do. What could people like Shaqueel Brown possibly want from a place like this once they'd exhausted the beauty and the weather?

'Don't they get bored very quickly once they're stuck in their villas though?' I questioned.

'Not at all. They come here for one thing only: privacy. It's all they're after, and this place gives it to them. De Niro, Mariah Carey, all of them, they just want discretion. They want to do what they like doing, as much as they want to, without anyone finding out. So the parties in the hills are legendary. It's all behind closed doors. And the island authorities protect that fiercely. They're not going to look a gift horse in the mouth.'

I sat quietly for a moment, taking it all in. We were on expenses here through a British newspaper, via Jonathan Davies Associates. The paper had no idea exactly who was going to be doing their dirty work, but they were paying a hell of a lot of their money for the privilege. The information on Shaqueel Brown was obviously good.

'So how are we gonna get the pictures, Mr Raymont? You're the man with all the experience and all the information. And you've got a future as a tourist guide if the pictures ever start to dry up.'

He laughed.

'Well, you see the little shack down on the beach over there?' We were slowing down to turn into a dirt track off the only paved road on the island.

I looked down at a Caribbean paradise. A strip of blindingly white sand bordered the wooden hut, and the sea licked gently on to it, palm trees hovering above like natural, curving cranes providing shade in all the right places.

'Not everybody wants Anguilla to be a hotspot for gay love, however much money is spent by the ones who are at it. We've got someone on the inside at Brown's villa complex. He's waiting to talk to us right now, down there at Ed's Shack.'

Yet again I had to marvel at how Jonathan and Marcus came up with this stuff. The long arm of the British press stretched into all sorts of murky places, as Shaqueel Brown was about to find out.

27

Over the next few days, we chased Shaqueel Brown all over the island, making sure we never blew our cover, gathering information about his movements, watching him and his followers. We saw no sign of a lover, male or female. That was obviously something he was keeping carefully under wraps.

I was glad to be able to relax and not worry about being seen. Nobody would have recognised me here anyway – this place was way beyond even my own previous level of celebrity – although I had been sure to maintain my new short-haired look throughout my time working with Marcus and my clothes were planned carefully, so that I fitted in easily with a relaxed but working look of tailored shorts and shirts that people on the island seemed to wear during the day.

One of our stakeouts came at a tennis club in Shoal Bay West. From the local network Marcus had set up with mobiles and pagers, and paid-off staff in each of the few resorts, we had gained information that Brown would be playing a couple of sets in the morning. We headed up there and used fake ID to get past security. Becoming British government inspectors of tourism meant a very specific look for me, but Marcus could just about have passed himself off as a member of the British authorities even before this assignment started.

We stalked the tennis courts from an open position next to the beach.

'He's really gay?' I asked, quietly. It was so disappointing. I could see how Brown had perpetuated the myth of being a heterosexual stud. He was gorgeous. His body was toned to perfection, rippling muscles under his tight white tennis shirt doing plenty for me, despite what I knew.

'As a Mexican tablecloth, apparently. His current squeeze is up at the villa now. What we have to do is get something with them clearly together. Obviously the kiss would be ideal, but holding hands would be money, as would touching faces. It's not going to be easy though. The only way we're going to do it is to get into the villa itself, and I'm working on some connections.'

I watched Shaqueel Brown take a swing at a fast serve from his opponent, and see the ball off into the right-hand corner of the court.

'He's good, isn't he? These people are good at everything? It makes you sick.' I laughed, quietly. Somebody probably used to say the same thing about me.

'Well, they are good at a lot of things, but there's always a chink in their armour. And no matter how hard they try, we'll always find it and expose it.'

I turned to look backwards towards the sea, giving the

impression that we were surveying the whole of the area, not just Brown's body.

'Do you ever feel bad about any of this? I mean, so the guy's gay. What's wrong with that?'

Marcus squinted in the same direction as me. He'd left his sunglasses in the car to present a more open impression to anyone who saw or challenged us. He didn't want anyone to think we had something to hide.

'Absolutely nothing. But the question of his sexuality isn't actually the point. You should think of it like one of those video games my nephew plays. People like Shaqueel Brown are playing the celebrity game, and we're just the obstacles they have to get over, the little meanies who want to spoil everything. They keep putting themselves up for it, so that they make more money and get more famous. And we're there to keep them in line. Especially if they get famous by pretending to be girl-hungry sex machines who then turn out to be gay. Shaqueel Brown is dishonest, pure and simple.'

I added some random notes to the clipboard I was carrying. Marcus was right, I guessed, though I pushed the hypocrisy of our behaviour firmly to the back of my mind.

'I know what you mean,' I said, as convincingly as I could. 'His whole career is based on a lie, that's true.'

My momentary doubts evaporated as quickly as they had formed. It only took a moment's thought about my own fall from grace to know I would do anything that was necessary to get it all back.

'Do you want to know how this whole thing started?

Why there were suspicions?' Marcus always had something up his sleeve.

I looked expectantly at him.

'It's because there had been no proper "kiss and tell" stories at all. Very odd. Every celebrity has women crawling out from under the floorboards to tell her story after she's slept with him, or hasn't. When stories like that came out about Shaqueel Brown, they always turned out to have emanated from those close to Brown, and that was very suspicious.' Marcus turned again to look down the coastline towards a rocky peninsula, before noting something on his clipboard. 'The guy was putting the stories out himself to prove something, but they just seemed to make him look better each time. Normally at least a few stories like that would be negative.'

'So he's been planting his own good publicity?' I scraped my foot across the ground, suggesting I was checking the quality of the earth in this part of the island. I was running out of government inspector behaviour ideas. We'd have to go soon.

'Yeah, and it raised a lot of questions in a few particular minds, along with some good intelligence that Jonathan was able to uncover. It only raised questions in very quick and perceptive minds though, and that's why we're here, because nobody else has a sniff of the story yet.'

I turned towards him.

'We need to go. I'm not very good at being a tourism inspector. I need to take some pictures.'

Marcus laughed and agreed.

'Tonight we take pictures undercover, background stuff for the main story but not the centrepiece. That'll come later if we can get into the villa.'

By the end of the night we had two hundred images of Shaqueel Brown on the street, in a restaurant in Maunday's Bay and getting into his own 4x4 to drive home afterwards. It was all part of the story, but from the mixed group of twelve that he was with, it was impossible to know if any of them was his gay lover.

We followed them back to the villa entrance, and at one o'clock in the morning I found myself at the foot of a large cliff, having walked half a mile up through pitch black, steamy Caribbean undergrowth. I could see the underneath of a balcony, but beyond that, there was no angle to catch even a glimpse of anybody that was in the villa that backed into the hillside above it.

We trudged slowly back to the car and got in.

'It's going to be difficult, but we'll do it. If we can do this, we can do anything, Natalie.'

I sighed heavily. I had faith, but it wasn't going to be easy. I became aware of a heavy silence in the car.

'You're very beautiful, Natalie.' Marcus turned towards me as he breathed out his words into the clammy wet heat of the night air and placed his hand on my leg. He squeezed, before moving it a little further up my thigh.

My whole body froze. I couldn't believe what was happening.

'Please take your hand off my leg right now,' I said

through tightly clenched teeth.

There was a momentary stand-off. Marcus's hand stayed where it was.

'Come on, don't tell me you're not the tiniest bit interested in a bit of Raymont?'

I snorted, trying to play down my feelings of revulsion and panic.

'Marcus,' I said calmly. 'There is no possibility that our working relationship will ever develop into anything else. Now, please remove your hand from my leg.'

I spoke steadily, hoping I was not betraying my true feelings. He was a man I thought I could trust. I realised how naïve I had been.

He removed his hand slowly.

'Thank you.' I breathed an inward sigh of relief and attempted to be breezy and play down the whole thing. 'Now let's get on with the job, shall we?'

There was silence in the car as we made our way home through the darkness. Our relationship dynamic had changed, but I would not let it affect the way I did this job. Marcus wouldn't try again anyway, I was pretty sure of that. He was a chancer, just like in his work, and he'd taken advantage of the darkness, how close we had become in our work, and the relaxation of the previous few days. Still, now that he knew I was not interested in any other type of partnership than work, I wondered how he would behave.

Not that it bothered me that much. I wasn't going to let anything get in the way of what I had to do.

28

Over the next two weeks our work crawled to a halt. It seemed we were getting nowhere. We photographed Shaqueel every day: at the small local stores, in this or that restaurant, running around the beach playing American football, but there was no hint that we could get closer, and take the pictures that we really needed. We knew we would have to get inside the villa, but we had no good leads.

Gradually, Marcus and I started to try and behave normally again, but I was definitely wary of him now. When we were not working, which was starting to be most of the time now, I hung out in my hotel room, hardly going to the pool any more in case he was there. I had a net connection and my laptop, and I was relieved to be able to connect with the outside world, away from the surreal life I had started to lead on the island, chasing a world-famous singer and conscious that my partner had wanted more from me than I was prepared to give him.

I felt lonely. For the first time in months, I wasn't sure where I was going and how I was going to get there. It had all been so easy so far with Marcus. He'd shown me so much about how to do this job, and he'd been at my side whenever I needed advice. Now he was distant, as if I had been the one to blame for his behaviour.

I started thinking about my mum and dad. A couple of times I tried to call, but as usual, the phone went to the answer machine. I left messages and numbers, but they didn't call back.

I thought about calling Jonathan and opting out of the assignment, but it wasn't a serious idea. What would I do when I went home? Sure, I had the money to pay him back now, or at least I thought I did, though there was doubtless some clause in our contract that said I would have to pay back anything he'd given in expenses if I didn't complete the assignment. He'd also been paying my expenses the whole time I lived in Bayswater. I hadn't been in a position to ask for a breakdown of my accounts. I knew it was likely that even though my debts were cleared, there wasn't going to be much left over if I quit now, and then I would be back to square one, this time with nowhere to live.

One empty afternoon, when we'd nothing new to know or photograph about Shaqueel Brown, I sat in my room and started to cry. It just came flooding out. I don't know what started it, except that I felt completely alone, and for the first time, that seemed to matter.

Later on I went online, and was excited to see Ravi's name on my MSN list of online contacts. It had been a long time since we'd spoken directly, although we'd emailed a few times since I'd been out of the country, but I needed to talk to him right now and I took the plunge. He'd always been there for me in the past, and there was no reason why he shouldn't be now, surely?

IMAGEGrrl: Are you OK Rav?

RaviBUFF: Hi Nat! Surprise or what? I'm good thanks yeah.

IMAGEGrrl: So what's new? How's your exams going?

RaviBUFF: They're all finished babe. In the bag. Haven't stopped for six months and now I've got nothing to do but wait!

IMAGEGrrl: I know the feeling. Do you think you did OK?

RaviBUFF: I think I'll get in. Should get my grades at least.

IMAGEGrrl: So what are you gonna do with your time?

RaviBUFF: Not a lot. There's a wedding coming up in the family, so that'll take up a bit of the summer, probably most of it knowing my family. But apart from that I'm just chilling. What about you?

IMAGEGrrl: Still in Anguilla.

RaviBUFF: Lucky cow. I dream of going to place like that. Sun, sand and sea and all paid for. You must be loving it. How's the job though?

IMAGEGrrl: The whole thing isn't as good as it

sounds. The job isn't going well and there's not a lot to do. And my partner's been misbehaving.

RaviBUFF: What do you mean?

IMAGEGrrl: Trying it on a bit. I thought he was sound, but he's been a bit of a perv. Nothing I can't handle tho, trust me.

RaviBUFF: Oh you poor love. Sounds like in Year Ten with that guy at the club in town. Remember? You punched him in the balls and he ran away?

I thought back to the night he was talking about. It seemed like a lifetime ago and the girl he described didn't seem like she could be me. I wondered how she would have dealt with Marcus.

IMAGEGrrl: How could I forget! It's so great to hear you, Rav.

And just like that, the images on the screen started swimming as my eyes filled up again. I missed Ravi, I missed some proper human contact as well. I couldn't be a machine the whole time.

RaviBUFF: Here's a hug from me:

A tiny icon of a little brown boy with his arms out in a hug shape popped up next to his name. I laughed, even though my nose had started to run. I wiped it quickly and tried to regain my composure.

IMAGEGrrl: I wish it was a real one.

RaviBUFF: Awww. You know I would if I could, darling. What's up with the job? Why's it not going well?

Obviously Ravi knew nothing about the assignment I was on. I had told him in an email that we were working undercover, and he hadn't asked any more. I got the impression he didn't really want to know.

IMAGEGrrl: It's just not going anywhere at the moment. We've been here nearly three weeks and we've not got any good leads yet. It's just day after day of sitting and waiting for a break. I've got nothing to do either.

There was a pause as we both let our fingers rest for a moment. As I did, I had a brainwave. What if I could get Ravi out here to spend some time with me? Marcus would be stubbed out, but the way things were I was sure he'd just let me get on with it and I could reconnect with Ravi in some way. Maybe we could finally put all the bad stuff behind us. It wasn't like I had anything else to do, and even Marcus had said it could take weeks to work our way into the villa. And Ravi wouldn't have to know anything about the work part. He could just hang out at the hotel and we'd spend time together when we could.

I was excited.

IMAGEGrrl: What if I could get you out here for a bit Ravi? Would you come?

I figured that Ravi could afford the flight, and he could stay in my room easily. There were two huge double beds anyway.

RaviBUFF: Seriously? You mean it? I've got a bit saved up so I could get a flight if it's not too much?

IMAGEGrrl: Of course I mean it. If I can sort it, will you come? The money won't be a problem once you're here if you can pay for a flight, I'll look after you, so don't worry about that. I'd love to see you again. We could have a right laugh.

RaviBUFF: Well I'm up for it then. Totally. Oh my god. I can't believe it.

We talked for another hour and I made some calls on my mobile. Soon it was all arranged. Ravi would be there in forty-eight hours and at last I would have somebody I trusted to spend some time with. I couldn't wait.

I slept better that night than I had for months.

29

On Ravi's second night in Anguilla, we went to the hotel bar and got wrecked. He'd been jetlagged the first night, and during the next day we'd just spent time on the beach, people-watching and having a laugh at everyone else's expense, just like we used to do in the old days. It wasn't heavy, and I was glad.

Rav had been hoping to do some celebrity spotting and he wasn't disappointed. I'd almost forgotten how exclusive this place was, but his excitement soon reminded me. Everywhere you looked there were people you'd heard of, or people who looked like you should have heard of them, judging by their incredible clothes, jewellery or perfectly toned bodies.

The hotel bar overlooked the Caribbean Sea and an incredible blood-red sunset was perfect for getting drunk to. We'd been there for a couple of hours when Marcus joined us. I found Ravi's attitude towards Marcus quite funny. They had briefly met in the hotel lobby when Ravi had arrived and both of them had offered a pathetically small greeting to the other. One couldn't care less and the other was openly hostile.

Ravi never could get all that macho stuff right, but his heart was always in the right place. He was polite, despite telling me earlier in the day that he'd love to knock Marcus out. I'd like to have seen him try. He was like a Twiglet on the beach in his shorts.

'So what do you make of our beautiful prison then, Ravi? Do you approve?' Marcus seemed a little bit tipsy himself. He must have been clearing out the minibar in his room again.

Ravi sucked in his breath and looked around him quizzically. 'What's not to like? Although from what Nat says, the job is making things a bit difficult to enjoy. Lots of frustration?'

Marcus laughed. 'Yeah, plenty of frustration.' He seemed to pick the moment that Ravi wasn't looking to confirm with a pointed eyebrow in my direction that it was not the job he had been referring to.

He picked up his cocktail and indicated it with a nod of the head.

'There are perks though, eh?' He took a deep suck on his straw and half the bright red liquid disappeared from the glass.

We were quiet for a moment. I could see Ravi staring at a guy across the bar from us at a table on his own. He was so obvious. He'd never learned to hide his feelings, because he'd had so few chances to practise in St Albans. His tongue had been hanging out for most of the day, looking at the male bodies on the beach. He wasn't used to this sort of display of gorgeous men, and he was obviously finding it hard not to ogle them now.

Marcus picked up the same signal. 'Like what you see around here?' He smirked at Ravi and then across at the guy at the table with a raised eyebrow.

Ravi jerked his attention back, a reflex action I'm sure. He must have done it a million times to try to avoid people finding out about his sexuality in that way. He blushed a little and wrapped his hands around his glass.

'Whatever.'

I didn't know what to say. It wasn't my place to defend Ravi to anybody, not that he even needed defending, but I felt for him. And Marcus was a piece of work sometimes. I wasn't going to let him get away with anything that hurt my best friend, no matter that we had to work together.

'Marcus, why don't you go and play on your own with the sharks or something?'

'Ohh, there's a bit of the old Natalie de Silva spark coming out again. I thought you'd lost it completely these last few days. Good to have you back, Nat. I'm glad Jonathan thinks it's OK for you to have your . . .' he paused for emphasis, 'lovely friend here to keep you company, but I've got a job to do. And while you've been sunning yourself and sitting on your arse for the last God knows how long, I've been working on our contacts. And I think it's about time you started to help.'

Marcus was more drunk than I'd thought. He was

slurring his words and had pushed his face up close to mine as he spoke.

I could sense Ravi's body tightening up next to me and I moved slightly towards him to avoid Marcus's alcoholic breath.

I faced Marcus down.

'I'll do whatever I have to do, but you're the one who gets the information, you know that's the way it works. You're the one with the contacts, Marcus, so don't have a go at me if you're failing your side of it.'

'You think you're so perfect, don't you? Well let me tell you . . . Natalie,' Marcus pronounced my name as if it was a product of a dog's arse. 'There's a hell of a lot more to this than meets the eye. And you need to get yourself focused, away from one gay boy to another.'

I reeled away from him. It must have been the drink talking, and his macho pride, because I'd never heard Marcus talk about anybody we were chasing in such a way. They were usually just targets to him, nothing else, not even people.

'I don't know if you're drunk or what, Marcus, but that's totally out of order. Apologise now.' I hoped he would, because I could feel Ravi beginning to rise behind me, the drink mixing with his already strong dislike of Marcus.

'Apologise? I've nothing to apologise to anybody for. Fuck you and your pretty boy from home. You need to work out your priorities, and right now that means exposing all the arse bandits round here for what they are.'

'Who the hell do you think you are?' Ravi shouted and rose off his bar stool.

From around the bar, faces turned in our direction. The bartender stopped and waited, perhaps wondering if he was going to have to intervene in a fight. I wondered too. I'd never known Ravi to be so animated.

'Nobody you need to know about. Natalie knows what she has to do. And I suggest she concentrates on it now, with no distractions.'

Marcus slid off his stool and strode out into the darkness beyond the fringes of the straw-roofed bar. I watched him go with some alarm. Ravi was left standing, the look on his face one of pure hatred. But Marcus had been very threatening. I hated him for the way he had talked to Ravi, but what if he spoke to Jonathan about this? What if they threw me off the job? I had nothing to go back to. That wasn't an option for me.

Ravi turned and looked at me.

'What did he mean, Nat? Tell me. What's going on?'

I didn't want to tell him anything, but I couldn't hide it now. He had a right to know.

'We're in a sting operation here, Ravi. We're after pictures of a guy who pretends he's straight, but in reality he's gay. It's no big deal. Just another assignment with somebody lying to protect themselves.'

I hadn't even considered what Ravi would think of this job. It had never crossed my mind that he would find out. But just at that moment, it hit me.

'You're outing somebody against their will?' Ravi seemed to crumble in front of my eyes, his anger not masking his horror. 'After everything you've seen in my life, everything I have to do to protect myself in case somebody finds out? All the lies?'

I grasped his shoulders as he refused to look into my eyes.

'It's a job, Ravi. It's all I've got. I have to do it. I haven't got anything else now.'

Ravi slowly raised his eyes to meet mine.

'And I guess you're acting under orders too, Nat? Like the Nazis when they gassed the Jews? Get a life, girl. You're kidding yourself.'

I stared into his eyes, but all I saw was anger. I looked away, unable to hold his gaze any longer.

I didn't see him speak, but I heard his words before he walked away.

'You make me sick, Natalie.'

30

Two days later we got our ticket to Shaqueel Brown's inner circle at Eden Villa. Ravi had left as soon as he could get a flight, and I was alone again. I knew I was letting Ravi down, but I couldn't think of any other way to get back what I wanted. It was a no-win situation, and Ravi was the first to lose.

Our passport to the villa had been staring us right in the face all the time. It was so obvious that nobody had thought of it. In the end, Jonathan had come up with the answer, after Marcus had all but given up. It had been a terrible couple of days between us, and I hated him for what he had done to Ravi, but once the plan came through, we both slipped straight back into our professional roles. It was no time for personality clashes to get in the way.

The world-renowned fashion photographer David St Vincent, who did a lot of work for JD Associates, was on the island, part of a group of celebrities and their retinues who were partying at the villa complex in San Quentin Bay. They were also attending private parties at Eden, where Brown was staying, in the heart of his inner circle. That circle was squared by our favourite publicity guru himself: I'd been photographed several times for British magazines by St Vincent, so it was a simple matter of Jonathan calling in a favour to get me into the villa as part of his group. And so the plan was set.

Marcus was still able to provide some extra information from a contact in the local government offices. By sunset, we had a floor plan for the recently built villa from the building regulations department. Marcus made me memorise the rooms that appeared most likely to be hiding anything. We figured the bathrooms, the kitchen and the living and dining areas were out, as was any other downstairs space, so any potential private areas were likely to be upstairs, and well out of the way of the shared spaces for guests.

In fact, there appeared to be two rooms that had no purpose at all. Could they be why Shaqueel Brown had chosen this villa? A place to hide secrets within an already totally discreet island hideaway?

It was eleven at night when we finally got to Eden. We'd spent the evening at Oliver's Restaurant, and eaten fabulous seafood caught fresh on the beach that day. It was a wonderful night, and I remembered exactly why I was doing this assignment. I wanted this back. It was mine. These American celebrities had no real idea of who this English girl was in their midst, but I milked the contacts for all they were worth, safe in the knowledge that David St. Vincent had been briefed to cover for me.

My main problem was the cameras. Marcus had decided

that I needed to use the latest micro cam, as we had done at the royal party. We would lose some picture quality, but the images would be clear enough. Lucky for me that the fashion for big lumpy handbags was still happening. I was able to get everything in there, including my mobile and my make-up.

I was introduced to Shaqueel Brown as soon as I arrived, his face betraying no confusion or doubt when David St Vincent called me a rising starlet and model with movie contracts coming from all directions. I smiled to myself. If that had been true I wouldn't have been fiddling about in the incredible marble bathroom of this villa, making sure the equipment was ready and working properly; I would have been out there sampling the high life again. In fact, all I could think about was getting the picture and not letting anybody down.

Soon I was left standing to one side and able to observe the group as a whole. There were about thirty people present, and they were swallowed up by the enormous interior of the luxury villa. In fact, the balcony terrace alone could have held three times as many as were there. I went outside and felt the strange sensation of knowing that Marcus was a hundred feet below me, ready to help in whatever way he could, if I needed him. I couldn't imagine how he could, given the circumstances and the location of the building on the side of a sheer mountain, and I didn't want to need any help from that man anyway. I wanted to do this on my own.

I had deliberately moved away to stand on my own. It had always got me attention in the past, when I wanted it.

'How you doin,' hon?'

A large black guy wearing a black suit and wraparound sunglasses, despite the fact that it was after midnight and pitch black outside, offered me a fresh cocktail. I hadn't noticed that I'd finished the last one, but I must have been nervously knocking back alcohol since I had arrived. He was clearly a minder, one of the men I'd seen in the pictures Marcus had shown me on the first day I'd arrived, but obviously part of the group as well. Brown appeared to treat all his minders as his best friends anyway.

'My name is Leroy. Is there anything else I can get you tonight?'

I smiled at how polite he was. It was such a contrast to his bulky, macho-looking exterior. His voice was like warm honey.

'No, I'm fine, really. I'm just enjoying people-watching. You know how it is.' This seemed like a good opportunity to get right into the inner circle. I decided to play it for what I could.

I tried to remember how to say absolutely nothing and just look good. It was the first rule of being a celebrity. If one of Brown's bodyguards wanted to get to know me better, that might give me some kind of way in and I wasn't going to let that opportunity go.

'Sure do. I'm enjoying doin' just that right now.' He smiled again. I attempted my best coy blush, hoping it didn't come out more like unflattering rosy cheeks.

We talked for a few more minutes, moving inside on our own and settling down on big comfy leather sofas overlooking the lights of the tiny bay down the valley in front of the house. I offered Leroy just the right amount of encouragement to keep him interested. All the old techniques were coming back now.

As I looked across at the rest of the group, Shaqueel detached himself and made his way back into the main body of the house. I wondered where he was going. Maybe he had gone to the loo? Did R 'n' B superstars go to the loo?

It was a good time to try and get a good look around this place. Maybe I would get what I was looking for, without trying too hard.

'I'd love to see the house, Leroy. It's so beautiful here. Would you show me around a little?' It was amazing what lengths I was prepared to go to.

'Of course, Natalie. Most of our guests get the guided tour on their first visit. They don't always get my version though.' He winked and I smiled. He was a cuddly bear of a man and I felt a twinge of guilt about leading him on. Unlike Marcus, he seemed to be the real thing.

I allowed Leroy to take my arm as soon as we were out of the main living area. Eden was pure, incredible luxury from one room to the next. I'd expected it to be amazing, but even knowing it came in at tens of thousands of dollars a night I was still blown away. There was a private gym with enough workout equipment to keep a professional basketball team fit. The next room contained a walk-in sauna with integrated sound system, a steam room, a swimming pool that was half inside the building, half outside, snaking its way back out and underneath the living area. There was a Jacuzzi with a computerised light show that would be the envy of many big London clubs, a fully equipped home cinema for up to forty people and best of all for me, the master bedroom with its panoramic view across the whole of the western half of the island and cameras and telescopes inset into the balcony to catch the sunset. We finished our tour there, quite deliberately I'm sure on the part of Leroy, a full twenty minutes after leaving the rest of the group. There was a massive Emperor bed, large enough for Shaqueel to romp with any number of his adoring fans, which I now knew he didn't like to do. We were so far away from the main part of the house now that I couldn't hear anything apart from crickets chirruping away outside the fly screens.

I managed to remember what I was there for.

'So Leroy, what would Shaqueel say to spending some time with me in here right now? Is he lonely up here in this big bed all by himself?' I tried to give it my best Marilyn Monroe. I knew what I wanted from Leroy, but it wasn't what he had in mind.

He laughed.

'I'm sure he'd like that a lot, Missy, but you've picked the wrong night. He's got a visitor of his own tonight, if you know what I mean.' He winked again. 'I think you'll have to make do with a roll on there on your own. Or we could test it out together if you'd like?'

He remained rooted to the spot. I'd managed to hook up with the enormous minder who was actually a shy guy with a few weak lines and a lack of killer confidence. Thank God, I thought to myself.

I sat down on the bed and stretched out, my short black dress rising up my thighs a little.

'I'd love to wake up in a bed like this. She's a lucky girl.' I deliberately drank off the last of my cocktail. 'Oh no. I've run out. Leroy, could you get me another? I could doze off in here.' I scooted further up the bed and kicked off my shoes. 'I'll try to still be awake when you get back.'

Leroy looked confused for a moment, before his face cleared.

'OK, I'll get you one. Don't move. I won't be two minutes.'

'Oh and I've left my shrug downstairs somewhere, near where we were sitting. A brown fur one. Could you find it for me? It's a little chilly with the windows all open up here.'

Leroy nodded enthusiastically and headed for the door.

'I'll get it for you, hon, you just make yourself comfortable and we can get you warm when I get back.'

I knew that my stole would be hard to find. I hadn't brought one with me.

As soon as he left the room I jumped up. I figured I would hear Leroy making his hefty way up the backstairs by which we had reached this place. I needed to find anything I could and quick. Most of all I needed to find Shaqueel Brown, and if I did, I felt sure that I would find his partner.

I tried a couple of closet doors and drawers, thinking there might be something incriminating in there that I could use. There was nothing but clothes. I had to find the rooms that we'd identified on the plans, but which Leroy had definitely not shown me on the tour.

I went out on to the landing and down the passageway, my bare feet making no sound on the bamboo flooring. I tried two doors. I knew one led to a guest bedroom, another to the weights room. Beyond the weights room was one of the secret rooms, which led out on to a private balcony. It might be my only chance.

The second door opened and I was in. Surrounded by weights and mats on the floor, I picked my way through the semi darkness and across to a window. Moonlight was flooding in, giving me at least a pathway of light to the hidden room. I could remember which wall was adjoining the secret room but there didn't appear to be a door. Was it just a walled-up piece of dead space after all?

Suddenly I heard a sound from the other side of the wall. It was a male voice. And then another. It must be Shaqueel Brown. It had to be. Who else would be in that room in the middle of a party, such a small gathering that everybody would notice, especially minders who had their minds on the job, if someone went upstairs who shouldn't.

I couldn't make out what was being said, but the voices definitely seemed to be coming from the window side of the wall. I looked out and tried to peer around the corner to see on to the private balcony that adjoined the secret room. But this house had been very well designed for privacy. The balcony was completely hidden. I knew it was there, and from what I could hear, there were low voices coming from the exact spot, but how was I to get to it?

Again, I searched for a handle or some kind of entrance to the secret room. I ran my hands up and down the wall, frantically searching. A minute had passed, maybe two. Even if Leroy gave me a special umbrella and extra fruit in my cocktail, I couldn't see him taking more than three minutes in total once he'd given up on finding the shrug.

Suddenly, my fingers felt a tiny switch, embedded into the flat skirting board above the bamboo floor. It wouldn't be a light switch, not there; it had to be something else, maybe something to do with the secret room. I took a deep breath, knowing that this was the moment of truth. The switch could set off a sound or floodlight system, or it could be what I was looking for. I flicked the switch down.

Incredibly, the wall started to move sideways, silently gliding on invisible tracks. I was terrified that whoever was on the other side would see it, so I flicked the switch again and the wall paused, leaving a gap about six inches wide. I crawled over to where light was spilling through the gap from the secret access, straight into the weights room in which I lay.

I peered around the wall and prayed for the first time in my life.

Through a double French door, out on a dimly lit wooden balcony, I saw Shaqueel Brown and another young man, arms around each other, gazing into the night. I pulled out my tiny camera and held it up to my eye.

'Come on,' I whispered, 'Give it to me, boys. Give it to me.'

As if on my command, Shaqueel turned to face his lover, straight into the full view of the lens of my camera.

And then they kissed passionately on the mouth.

I clicked the shutter button, once, twice, three times. Then I clicked again, four, five times for good luck, pushing myself not to run, my fingers crossed as time hung by a thread and I prayed I could get out of there in one piece, with enough evidence to close the deal.

I flicked the button on the skirting board upwards and the wall slid shut. In seconds I was back on the bed in the master bedroom, in time to slip my camera into my handbag and graciously take a long, cool Tequila Sunrise from a grinning and apologetic Leroy's outstretched hand.

31

I got a text from Marcus when I woke up the next day, saying we would be going home tomorrow and that my plane ticket was at reception. I didn't expect a more personal service from him. We had become almost silent assassins in our work, barely communicating unless it was absolutely necessary for the job. There was nothing personal or friendly left in our relationship at all since the Ravi incident in the bar.

Anyway, the job was done and there was no reason to stay any longer, or talk to Marcus at all. I couldn't wait to go. Tomorrow I would be able to relax for the first time in weeks, get back to my flat in Bayswater, close the door on Jonathan, Marcus, paparazzi photography and everything else and forget it all for a while, at least until the next job. Maybe this would be the last time I had to do this. Maybe Jonathan would have already started the process of my rehabilitation with the media that he had been promising to do since he'd given me this assignment.

I'd had a good night's sleep and woken up quite early, around eleven, considering I'd only got to bed at five o'clock in the morning, after we'd finally downloaded the photographs and emailed them off to London. The story would break while I was flying home. By the time I landed at Heathrow, the newspapers would be full of my pictures and I would start earning money. I should have felt relief, but I had a nagging sense that I'd lost a lot, as well as gaining so much.

After some pastries from room service and a long cool bath, I decided to go out and do some 'real' photography, all around the local area, of people, places and things. I left my mobile in the hotel room so I wouldn't be disturbed for once and spent the rest of the afternoon on the trail of every beautiful angle I could find. And I found a lot. It was an incredible feeling, pointing the camera at something gorgeous, something only I could see. Something that I could use in a positive way, to enrich people's lives, not ruin them. I was used to my subjects being targets. At least for now I was taking pictures with permission.

I'd missed this. It was something that was in my heart, and I wished I could do it so much more, but I knew that if I wanted to continue with the life I used to have, I needed to keep working with Jonathan. And anyway, I wanted it. I loved the excitement that had stirred in me in that weights room last night. It was amazing, like every encounter in my work with Marcus. And until the press had forgotten my past behaviour and I could get back some kind of life in the limelight again, I could live with this, this hidden, secret existence in the shadows of real life. I was good at it, really good. After the success of the night before, I knew that I would be in demand, we both would, and I could definitely demand more money next time. Maybe being a pap was my future after all?

When I got back to the hotel, I had voicemail. It was Jonathan, his rough-edged Aussie tones immediately recognisable as soon as he started talking.

'Natalie, give me a call. I need to talk to you urgently.'

That was it. No congratulations on a job well done. I was a bit miffed, but then Jonathan wasn't exactly a fountain of feelings. I guessed there must be another job that I had to get to immediately. I groaned inwardly. So much for some time to rest. I called Marcus's room to see if he knew what was going on.

There was no answer.

I called his mobile number, but the line was dead, so I tried reception.

'Hi there, this is Natalie Bayliss in room 349, I'm trying to contact Marcus O'Brien in 252.' The change in surnames had been our little joke when we arrived.

'Yes Miss Bayliss, Mr O'Brien has checked out. He left for the airport this morning for the 9 a.m. flight. Could I help you with anything else?'

I thanked the receptionist and replaced the receiver, before sitting down on my bed, puzzled. I'd assumed he'd be on the same flight as me. Why would Marcus leave without telling me he was going? I'd expected a text at least.

Immediately I speed-dialled Jonathan's number in London.

'Jonathan, it's me, how's it going?'

I expected some kind of thanks for what I'd done, before he launched into the urgent message, but there wasn't any of that.

'I'm OK, Natalie. Did you get your tickets? Marcus left them at reception for you.'

'Yep, I picked them up when I came in. I just found out he's left already. What's going on? Is there a new assignment?'

There was never any small talk between Jonathan and me any more, and I could sense that today he wanted to get to the point of whatever it was that he had to say, more than he ever had, but he was being unusually short with me, even for him.

'No, no, there's no new job. Marcus had to leave for other reasons.'

I was more confused now. Marcus had no life apart from work. What other reasons could there be? Why was Jonathan being so weird when I'd just provided him with the biggest scoop of his whole career?

'Where's he gone? What's going on, Jonathan?'

Something wasn't quite right here.

'You'd better sit down and listen, Natalie. You have a lot to take in.'

I did as I was told, like some kind of machine. I had the feeling that I wasn't going to like what I had to hear.

'Go on,' I said, quietly, taming the sickness that was gathering in my stomach.

'Very well, I'll give it to you plain. I know you prefer plain speaking, as I do. I'm terminating your contract with me completely today. You have tickets to get home. You will be paid the agreed rate for last night's work. After that our business together is closed. Your possessions from the flat are already in storage at a facility in London, and you will have access to them five days from now. You are not to go back to the Bayswater flat. It has already been reassigned. Do you understand?'

I felt my insides start to turn to liquid, but I tried to come out fighting.

'What the hell . . . what do you mean? I've just given you a great story. What do you mean, terminating?'

I tried to focus on the minimalist woollen rug beside the bed and keep my head from spinning me over.

'Just what I say. There are reasons, and they will all become clear over the next couple of weeks. For now, though, you need to understand this: you've outlived your usefulness for me, Natalie, and you're no longer a part of my organisation.'

'Why? What have I done wrong? I don't understand.' A detached part of me, floating above the situation and watching what was happening, wanted to burst into tears. But inside, I could only feel anger and resentment building instead.

'It's not about you, it never was. It's about what I wanted from this. I've got what I wanted. Marcus and I have been working together for a long time, Natalie. You should have thought about that. Why would I want some discredited celebrity to take pictures with one of the finest paps in the business? Think about it. The guy couldn't get a job because of his past. What's the best way to get rehabilitated by the press?'

I hadn't a clue what he was talking about. I couldn't believe what I was hearing.

He went on, coldly.

'I'll tell you how. You do a good deed, tell them, or show them, something they want to hear. Tomorrow, your pictures will try to destroy the life of a very popular entertainer, a loved and respected singer. But we're living in the twenty-first century and unfortunately for you, the stories that go with the pictures will take his side. The press will compare the photographer to scum, and they'll name names. Or rather, they will name one name. Natalie de Silva. Because they will also have an article by the formerly disgraced paparazzi photographer, Marcus Raymont, who will tell the whole story of how he tried to get you to change your ways, how he even opted out of your plan to set up Shaqueel Brown when he couldn't stop you, and how you went to the villa alone to get your pictures last night. He'll explain how he has learned from his past, but you clearly haven't.'

He stopped for a split second. I felt like I couldn't breathe.

'Why are you doing this to me? What have I ever done to deserve this?' I could hardly speak. My words were coming out in fragments.

'Because you're expendable. Because I can. Just like I

pulled the plug when you stopped doing as you were told. As soon as I saw you in those pictures with Jamie O'Brien I decided to get rid of you. God knows I had plenty of other pretty girls queuing up to take your place. That's what you people don't understand. You're not famous because of anything you are, it's because we choose to make you, and now I've chosen to finally get rid of you.'

I couldn't quite take it all in. All I knew was that it was over. The whole thing.

'Marcus was one of us. And the newspapers have wanted him back for years, because he was the best. And we look after our own. So you're going to take the fall once again. It won't be pretty, Natalie, so I suggest you go home and lock all the doors. Or you could get yourself a publicist.'

He snorted loudly at his own joke.

'I haven't got anywhere to go. My parents won't let me come back. I —'

'You should have thought about that before you started believing in your own publicity. I did you a huge favour on New Year's Eve, but you couldn't leave it alone. So I signed you up as the fall girl for Marcus Raymont's return. A publicist's dream.'

I wanted to throw the phone at the wall and bury myself in the bed linen and never come out again, but I had to try to understand it all, whatever effect it had on me. I knew I would never speak to this man again and my future was his to destroy.

'What do you mean about New Year's Eve? What

favour did you do me? That was an awful night for me. I don't understand.'

'Natalie, you just don't understand anything. You've been in over your head since I signed you up for the *Sunday Newz* column and I've been pulling your strings ever since. The New Year's Eve stories came from me. I planted them deliberately. Obviously, your bad behaviour was useful, but by then I knew that you would help me with some kind of stupid, celebrity display of yourself. You'd been at it for a while by then. All I did was help you further down the pan with some carefully placed photographs and some well chosen words. You did the rest yourself.'

I couldn't bring myself to hear any more. I dropped the phone on to the crisp white sheets of my luxury hotel bed and rolled away into a ball, holding myself tightly as I cried. The mobile lay framed against the perfect purity of the linen like a hand grenade, black and threatening. Only it had already gone off in my hand.

I saw the light flick off as Jonathan ended the call.

32

It was early evening when I got finally got myself out of bed and out of the room. I hadn't been able to move for hours, everything spinning around inside my head. The sun was dipping behind the palm trees beside the hotel pool, and I needed to get out of the space I'd been cooped up in for so many hours.

I wanted to drink. I needed something to blur all the emotions and ease the pain. So I took myself to the hotel bar and started knocking back vodka and lemonade, because it was sweet enough that I didn't notice the double shots of alcohol that were fizzing into my veins.

I tried calling Ravi, but he wasn't there. Then I called my parents, but it went straight to the machine. I left a message telling them that things had changed, I had changed, asking them if I could come home. This was what they had wanted me to do, wasn't it? I hoped that when they did hear it, they would want me back. It was a chance, a safety net, the one I'd always had. I prayed that it would still be there for me when I got back home to England.

I got through to Evie, but she refused to speak to

me. She had exams in the morning and didn't want to argue and couldn't understand how I thought she would even talk to me after the way I'd treated Ravi. Even my grandma wouldn't talk to me. She said she couldn't go against my parents in this and asked me to please not call again.

I even called Smooch, hoping that she could tell me that what Jonathan had said, at least some of it, wasn't true. When I heard her voicemail message I gave up. She sounded so happy, so alive. I couldn't bring myself to leave a message. After all, if what Jonathan had said was true, then Smooch must have been part of the set-up as well. He was her publicist too. I began to see how the whole thing had played out. I'd been completely screwed, virtually from the start.

Why hadn't I done the right thing in the first place and deleted those original pictures, just got rid of them? Everything would have been different. My friends would still be talking to me; my parents wouldn't have disowned me. I wouldn't be sitting drunk in a bar in Anguilla with nothing but my clothes and my cameras.

At least I still had my cameras. I looked down at my backpack, and fished out my favourite Nikon. I had talent, didn't I? I'd proved I had what it took to be a great paparazzi photographer. There were other agents and publicists out there, more editors, plenty more. I could still make some money from that, however disgusting it made me feel. What else could I do, anyway? They'd done this to me, so I would keep doing it to other people and save myself that way. It was my only choice, the only thing I was capable of doing.

I charged the hefty bar bill to my room in a final gesture of defiance to Jonathan, and walked away unsteadily on to the moonlit Caribbean beach. It was a beautiful night. It always was here. No wonder the stars came here for their privacy. That would all be blown away tomorrow morning. They would realise that the paps could get them anywhere now. Things had moved on to another level. Natalie de Silva had moved things on to another level.

I took off my sandals and splashed gently into the tiny waves that were breaking on to the wet sand. It was a warm sea, and it felt wonderful on my naked feet, alive, free. If only I could feel so free.

I strolled on a couple of hundred metres further, around a few jagged rocks and some hidden pools, picking my way through the moonlit sands well away from any human life, until I came to the edge of another bar area, more exclusive than the one at my hotel, partly because it was inaccessible from anywhere except from the beach, partly because it was owned by an Arab sheikh who valued his privacy.

I stopped in the shadowed darkness away from the bar itself and watched the sights and sounds that used to be a part of my life as well: glasses clinking together in vague toasts to nothing in particular, the occasional tinkle of a woman's laughter piercing the general hubbub of conversation, music set to a level that didn't interrupt the important, empty sentences coming out of the mouths of the stars. It was all just as I remembered it, just in a more beautiful setting.

Perching on a rock, half-hidden from the bar itself, I took out my camera, finding the correct zoom so that I could focus in on individual faces. It was a game I used to play when I was little, a test I set myself: how to zoom in on unsuspecting people passing my house from my bedroom window, whilst trying to get a tiny mole on their face in focus, trying to get a picture that seemed to sum up its subject perfectly, that would say more with its detail than I could ever say in words.

I zigzagged across the bar area searching for interesting faces. I noticed a couple of well-known actors, beer bottles in hand, to the left. They were lost in conversation, clearly enjoying the night air and a few drinks. In front of the bar, on the sand, there was a mixed group, the women all dressed in flowing white cotton, the rich woman's choice of island clothing for its cool, sophisticated class. They were clearly debating whether to leave for the next exclusive venue of the night, or stick it out where they were. I could see every tiny wrinkle on each forehead. Perhaps they had heard of a better party, a better atmosphere somewhere else?

I moved the viewfinder to the right and pulled back to a wide-angled focus, finding another subject, a young woman in a tight red dress, crouched alone over a bench perched in some shadows quite a long way from the main area of the bar, where the beach met the tree line. She seemed to be anxious, casting glances here there and everywhere. It was obvious that she did not want to be seen, but she was safe for now in what was a relatively private space.

I focused more closely in on her face. It had a beautiful, pale, luscious aura. Even in the shadows it leapt out and grabbed you with its perfection. Her lips were full, her nose like a sculpted wedge of porcelain. This was a face I wanted to photograph. I tightened the viewfinder into extreme close-up, steadying myself by resting my right elbow comfortably into my thigh. As I became still, I caught a pair of staggeringly beautiful eyes as they flickered towards me, under heavy black lashes.

And that's when I recognised her.

Jennifer Jones – Jen – rising young model – known for her unconventional boyish beauty.

Suddenly I lost the eyes and they were replaced with hair. I pulled back the zoom and refocused slightly less closely. On the rugged bench in front of her were two white lines of powder. I'd seen enough of London nightlife to know exactly what it was and where it was going. Jen leaned in and falteringly drained the cocaine into her nostrils. Odd, but she looked awkward somehow. As far as I knew, Jen Jones was not into drugs – Class A or otherwise. But then, what did I know? I shrugged off the thought and, driven by instinct and the knowledge that I was watching the photographic equivalent of a stick of dynamite, I let off a volley of shots, catching her fully in the act.

As the last picture faded, I saw Jen look up, seemingly interrupted, and stare directly into my lens.

I stood up quickly to turn and retrace my steps. Maybe she hadn't seen me? I'd been in the shadows after all. I began to stride towards my hotel again, without looking back. I thought about how lucky I had been. Maybe life wasn't so bad after all? How could I complain when I was thrown such an incredible lifeline? Somebody up there must be looking after me, just as they had nearly a year before.

But then I heard Jen's voice from behind me.

'Excuse me,' she called out. 'Excuse me?'

I stopped, the sand scrunching up beneath my toes as I gripped them tightly against each other, and turned to face her. She was no more than a few metres away.

'Do you know who I am?' She appeared disorientated. I could understand why, drugs or no drugs.

I nodded. 'Obviously. Who doesn't?' I wanted to sound callous, to force her to leave me alone. I didn't usually get into conversation with my targets and I wasn't going to start now. It was an uncomfortable situation.

'Please, I heard you. Taking the pictures. I saw you.'

She sounded and looked terrified. I would have been too in her position. I could imagine exactly how she felt. She was wiping her nostrils as she spoke, almost unable to stand upright, and I thought she might collapse in front of me any second.

I lifted my camera again to refocus. Jen Jones snorting coke followed by Jen Jones collapsing? What a double whammy. I'd be set up for life.

'Oh my God – you're paparazzi, aren't you?'

She must have been deluding herself for a moment that I

was some kind of tourist taking pictures of her in the middle of the night.

I looked her directly in the eye and nodded. I had nothing to be ashamed of.

'Please. Please don't use those pictures. I beg you. This is not me – I mean, I'm not into drugs, it's my first time—' she stopped, shaking her head. 'Not that you're going to believe that. But it's the truth. I'm just going through some stuff . . . please don't do this.'

She reached out as if to take the camera itself from me.

I stared at this beautiful, desperate young woman before me. She was around my age, too – and like me she'd had all the breaks, because she was good at being pretty and good at wearing clothes, like I'd been good at taking pictures and whatever else people seemed to have decided about me. We were not so far apart in our experiences; we'd both been victims of control, and controlled others, too. And now I could destroy her, just like JD had tried to destroy me. I had power at last, control over my own destiny, for the first time in months.

'I'm begging you,' Jen's eyes were a mess of tears. 'Please don't do this to me.'

I had a simple choice: my future or hers. To be a somebody again, or to be a nobody. To take everything away from her and get everything back for myself.

I took a step away from her and raised the camera to eye level so that I could see the images I had taken clearly, masked from the light of the moon and the reflections from the ocean.

Jennifer backed away slightly and fell to her knees in the sand, her face crumpled into her chest. She began to sob, quietly.

I walked to where she was kneeling and lifted her face with my finger under her chin.

She looked up at me in confusion and fear. Her mascara was starting to dribble down her left cheek in a line. Surely I couldn't be so cruel as to take more pictures of her now, in this pathetic, defeated state?

And that's when it hit me. What kind of monster had I become? I knew more than anyone what it felt like to be destroyed, to see my life spiralling out of control. I had allowed greed, and selfishness, to dominate my world. If I carried on like this I'd wake up one morning, friendless and alone, hated.

I knelt down in front of her and grasped her hand in mine, placing it around one side of my camera. Together, we held on to it. She glanced at it fearfully, her eyes almost incapable of looking, terrified of the pictures I was trying to show her, of how I was rubbing her face into the hell she could be about to start living.

I forced to her to look at the camera, holding her by the shoulders to steady her gaze as I flicked through the images. When they were finished, I ejected the memory card from the side of the camera and shut it down. The lights went off and we were left bathed in the luminescent glow of the moonlight.

Jen turned her face towards me, watching the memory

card in my hand, her eyes betraying her terror.

'Please?' She begged, now silent, her fear paralysing her emotion.

I took her shaking hand again, folding the card into it, holding both her hand and the card so tightly that for a moment I could feel it digging into both of our fingers, creating an impression that would take several minutes to fade, an impression we would share. We were locked together like this for several seconds before I rose unsteadily to my feet, leaving her clutching the memory card on her own.

I glanced out at the rippling ocean and back at Jen Jones. She had clasped the hand containing the memory card so tightly to her chest that I thought she might never let it go. She started to sob again.

Turning back towards my hotel, I saw the bright lights ahead of me, and beyond them the darkness of the sky, and I began the long walk that would take me back to my future.

Turn over to read the

consequence

of this story...

consequences...

Runway Girl

Prologue

If it hadn't been for Stevie, I would never have been a model.
'YOU OWE IT ALL TO ME'; that's how he used to sign off
his texts to me. Six months ago the texts stopped. I should
have been glad; I used to complain about those texts, a lot.
Once, during a really complicated shoot for British *Vogue* (the
cast included three ballerinas balancing on horses and a small
band of acrobats; I spent three hours on a trapeze) he texted
me fifteen times: 'I'M BORED . . . THE DVD IS BROKE . . .
YOU OWE IT ALL TO ME' over and over again.

When I finally got down from the swing, I jabbed out a
single, furious reply: 'I'm working!!! Stop SHOUTING'. It
didn't occur to me that he might be missing me. Last night
on the beach, I would have given anything for one of
Stevie's rude, shouty birthday messages.

On my seventeenth birthday, I was being sown into a
white silk couture dress in a freezing car park in Berlin when
the assistant stylist handed me my phone: TOO OLD TO
BE JAIL BAIT, TOO YOUNG TO BE A WOMAN.
HAPPY BIRTHDAY FREAK XXX PS – YOU OWE IT
ALL TO ME.

He was right. You don't have to be beautiful to be a model, but you do have to be seen. If I'd never met Stevie, no model scout in the world could have discovered me. Without Stevie I would have spent the last two years sitting in my bedroom watching old Reese Witherspoon romcoms, wishing I was shorter, blonder, perkier.

Stevie said cute blonde girls were fine but he couldn't eat a whole one. He didn't so much build my self-esteem up, as tear the rest of the world down, until we were the only two people left standing. The pretty girls all the other boys at school drooled over were, according to Stevie, 'plastic' and 'obvious.' We were 'freaks,' which was a good thing. When the agency signed me, Stevie acted like the freaks had won, for all time: 'You seeeee' he crowed, 'Obvious doesn't cut it.'

I never pointed out to him that plenty of models are totally obvious; they're the prettiest girls at school only prettier. Some of these girls grow up liking what they see in the mirror so much they have to share it with the world; they walk through agency doors at fourteen and are signed on the spot; their mothers are ex-models, ex-actresses, ex-beauties. I was never one of those girls; my mother was never a beauty.

Growing up, I didn't exactly hate what I saw in the mirror; I just didn't expect anybody else to like it. A good day was a day when nobody stared. When I was fifteen I went through a phase of trying to disguise my height. 'You know, when you walk like that (head drooped forward, shoulders up round the ears) it makes you look like a hunchback,' quipped Stevie. 'You're tall. Only short-arse idiots have a problem with that.'

Stevie is only five foot four. He doesn't like to mention height – his or mine; it would have cost him something, using an expression like 'short arse'. I gave up on the Quasimodo thing. Stevie made me walk tall. He got me out of my bedroom. It's because of Stevie I was in the right place at the right time on my sixteenth birthday.

'It's your birthday. You're sixteen! We are going to the Oxford Circus Flagship TopShop.'

When Stevie refers to anything or anybody he truly respects, he always says their full name, with, sometimes, a bit of additional information. He started doing it round about the same time as the first series of The OC, so I guess he picked it up from Summer, and her not-at-all-annoying habit of calling the world's cutest geek 'Seth Cohen'. I didn't take much persuading; It was Saturday, it's not like I had anything else planned and, besides, I appreciated designer-inspired clothes almost as much as Stevie. I muttered something about having no money and couldn't we just watch a DVD, a bit of token resistance, just to give him the thrill of changing my mind.

'You are not spending your birthday in bloody Reading!' hissed Stevie.

'But I live in Reading, Stevie,' I said mildly, 'so do you.'

'Exactly!'

Six hours later I was standing in the vintage section of the

Oxford Circus Flagship TopShop with nothing to show for our day of fashion pilgrimage except dehydration (the only brand I truly cared about at that moment was Evian) and a large scratch on my cheek from one of the dozens of zips I'd hauled over my head. There are days when clothes cover you like excited puppies, and days when they droop, depressed, the moment you put them on. This was a day when the clothes were suicidal.

'I'm not buying it Stevie. Let's go. I've had it.' I shoved an inky-blue beaded dress back on the rail – a dress he had made me try on three times – and marched off. I expected a siren wail of protest to follow me but there was nothing. Sometimes Stevie lets you think he's given in, when, in fact, he's just re-grouping. I had my foot on the exit escalator when he grabbed my arm and yanked me back.

He hooked the dress (still on its hanger) over my head and barked: 'Look Freak, you don't have to show your stringy legs. Wear it over jeans – it will be totally fabulous. You'll look like Mischa Barton. From the neck down, anyway.'

'It's too short for me,' I pleaded, 'it will look like a blouse.'

'Exactly,' said Stevie.

I went back and bought the dress. That's why I was on the escalator, going up to the ground floor at 6.45pm instead of 6.30pm, just as Corinne Benson-Turner, head of new talent at Focus Model Management, was on the parallel downwards escalator.

'Hey! Yes, you, girl in the green jacket. Wait for me. I need to speak to you!' It was mortifying. Being spoken to by strangers was my least favourite thing in the world. (It really is amazing how often complete strangers come up to me to tell me that I am, like, tall.) I would have bolted but Stevie, who would never knowingly walk away from a scene, clamped his hand to my arm.

'She's acting like a psycho,' he trilled, delighted. I didn't trust myself to speak. It was my birthday, and my best friend, my only real friend, was forcing me to meet a madwoman.

'What's the worst that can happen?' Stevie whispered in my ear, as Corinne stepped off the escalator, looking flustered (she'd run up the steps) but not at all psycho.

'She probably wants to know where you got your fabulous jacket.' This seemed possible; my jacket – a charity shop find I'd taken apart and re-made on my aunt Pat's old sewing machine – was pretty damn fine. I'd shortened the sleeves to three-quarters length, and nipped in the waist to turn a seventies horror into fifties chic. I wondered if the crazy woman was going to try and buy my jacket. It had happened before: two months previously a woman came up to me in the Save the Children shop and bought the top I was wearing for twenty pounds; it was halterneck I'd made out of an old velvet curtain. I shivered all the way home, topless (in every sense) under my parka.

'Good, you're here. Thought I might have scared you away.' Corinne smiled brightly and I thought: you're pretty, like a model. Long brown hair, light golden tan (she was just back from a four day shoot in Mauritius, I found out later) and skinny. But not like-a-boy skinny like me; she was skinny with breasts.

'. . . So if you think you might be interested then come into the agency for a chat. I really think it will be worth your while. You've got something.'

'I've got a – a what . . . ?' I was so mesmerised by Corinne's lips – were they that colour naturally or had she found the best lipstick shade in the history of cosmetics? – that I barely heard what she was saying. Stevie, on the other hand, hadn't missed a thing. He wasn't just listening to Corinne; he was inhaling her.

'She wants to make you a model,' he squealed in my ear. 'She's from a proper agency and everything. Focus! I've heard of them. They discovered Veronique at Heathrow!' Corinne smiled that smile again.

'That's right. That was me actually, I spotted Veronique. She's doing very well for us.'

Veronique retired from modelling last year, aged twenty-two, to marry a minor British aristocrat and raise sheep in Buckinghamshire. But two years ago she was 'The Girl who put the Super back in Supermodel'; an old-fashioned eighties style beauty, all hair and legs and teeth, she was the ultimate Brazil beach babe. (In fact, she's from Liverpool, with a Scouse accent so broad even English photographers used to requested an interpreter.)

All this talk of Veronique made Corinne's show of interest in me even more bizarre. I sincerely doubted whether Veronique and I were the same species. Could the woman who had 'spotted' the superist super of them all really be saying that I could be a model? I scowled. Corinne put her hand on my arm and steered me and Stevie (who was still attached to my other arm) away from the escalator to a relatively quiet spot near a display of granny-style handbags.

'Are you OK?' she asked, gently.

'Is this a joke?' I snapped. Sometimes when I am nervous or upset I can be quite rude. This was one of those times.

'Not at all, I'm completely serious,' she took a business card out of a huge white handbag and pressed it into my hand, 'You have a great look. Come and see me, next week.'

'Oh, she will, she will,' panted Stevie, who seemed to be having difficulty breathing. 'Wednesday afternoon suit you?' he said, inexplicably, 'She can do Wednesday.' Corinne looked a little taken aback.

'Wednesday's fine.' And she smiled and was gone.

You know when something huge happens it can be hard to face up to it straightaway? The detail you can look at, but not the whole thing, not all at once; it's like you can't stand back far enough to take it all in. That's how it was on the train back to Reading. I spent the first ten minutes of the journey arguing with Stevie.

'We're at school on Wednesday, or had you forgotten that? I said irritably.'

'It's only double maths and games; we can skip it.' Stevie looked exasperated. 'I had to say *something*. You were acting like she'd just cancelled Christmas, not offered to make you a star. Focus Management are going to make you a model. In real life!'

'Come in for a chat she said, that's *all* she said, and now you've said I will, and I'll go and she'll realise she's made a mistake and it'll be awful and it'll be all your fault! You're always making me do things I don't want to and I'm sick of it!'

'You mentalist!' shrieked Stevie. A woman sitting next to him stood up suddenly, grabbed her little boy's hand and dragged him to the next carriage. This had the effect of shaming us into sullen silence. The rest of the journey I stared out the window, telling myself not to hope, trying not to believe it was possible, trying not to want anything at all.

Stevie sat so quietly it was as if all the excitement had been drained out of him. I thought: if we're not speaking then there'll be nobody, nobody I can talk to about this, this thing, this . . . me, being, maybe, a, model.

We got off the train in silence but just as we reached the exit Stevie put his arm round my waist. Immediately, I relaxed.

'Promise me you're going to go. To the agency? It doesn't have to be Wednesday. You don't have to take me. Just go.' His voice was low and serious. After my hissy-fit on the train I couldn't tell him that I had never seriously considered not going, that a part of me was afraid of how much I wanted to go.

So all I said was: 'Yes Stevie, I'm going – on Wednesday.

And you're coming too.' I'd never been to London on my own. I'd never been anywhere, much, without Stevie.

We went to McDonald's on the way back to mine. The bright plastic chairs looked even brighter and more plasticky than usual. I realise I had a headache.

'Let's eat in', said Stevie, 'dine in style. It's your birthday.' He ordered me a large Fillet O' Fish meal, a Sprite, a strawberry milkshake and a doughnut. He had the grilled chicken salad.

'Better make the most of it. After next week . . .' he grinned. 'You'll probably never be allowed to eat again.'

I wanted to ask him if he thought I really could be a model, but I couldn't get the words out; I didn't want to hear the neediness in my voice. So all I said was, 'I've got a bloody awful headache. 'Stevie fished an ice-cube out of his Sprite and ran it across my forehead. Cold sticky water ran down my nose.

'Look at you,' he said, 'the supermodel.'